PENGUIN BOOKS

# *Flacco's*
## Burnt
## Offerings

Flacco was conceived on the pages of animator P. J. Livingston's drawing board in 1985. Since then, Mr Livingston has been forced to abandon his life's work and succumb to the harrowing demands of Flacco, who has dragged the hapless animator across the planet, performing in festivals from Edinburgh to Montreal as Flacco attempts world domination via the diminutive Livingston.

Flacco appears regularly on 'Arts Today' on ABC Radio National and on radio Triple J.

Mr Livingston, when he can escape from Flacco's custody, has appeared in numerous film and theatrical productions.

# Flacco's
# Burnt
# ·Offerings

FOREWORD BY JOHN CLARKE
ILLUSTRATED BY P. J. LIVINGSTON

PENGUIN BOOKS

*Flacco would like to thank Julie Gibbs, Clare Coney, Michael Sherman, Rhonda Thwaite, Hilary Linstead and Associates, particularly the assiduous Anna McAllan and the assuaging Leisa James, John Clarke, The Sandman, Stephen Abbott, Mark Kennedy, Mikey Robins, Helen Razor and the JJJ juggernaut, Janne Ryan, David Marr and the Arts Today brigand.*

Penguin Books Australia Ltd
487 Maroondah Highway, PO Box 257,
Ringwood, Victoria 3134, Australia
Penguin Books Ltd
Harmondsworth, Middlesex, England
Viking Penguin, A Division of Penguin Books USA Inc.
375 Hudson Street, New York, New York 10014, USA
Penguin Books Canada Limited
10 Alcorn Avenue, Toronto, Ontario, Canada M4V 3B2
Penguin Books (N.Z.) Ltd
182 ~190 Wairau Road, Auckland 10, New Zealand

First published by Penguin Books Australia, 1995

10 9 8 7 6 5 4 3 2

Designed by Michael Sherman, Blow-Up Design
Photography by Rhonda Thwaite
Printed by Australian Print Group, Maryborough, Victoria

National Library of Australia
Cataloguing-in-Publication data:
Livingston, Paul
    Flacco's burnt offerings.

    ISBN 0 14 024782 3.

    1. Australian wit and humor. I. Title.

A828.302

Dedicated to
Stanley J. Livingston

# Contents

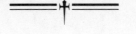

# FOREWORD
## BY JOHN CLARKE

Many readers will know Mr Livingston principally as the owner of a spectacular comic imagination driven by a performance gene which writes its own material.

His celebrated ability to free-fall and levitate simultaneously using only the conventions of logic and a language somewhat akin to English, has been witnessed and admired in theatres here and in both other countries.

He has also appeared in many of the wonderfully interesting films and television programmes which are such a feature of life in Australia.

But above all perhaps, listeners to radio will recognise that Mr Livingston has sustained a nation with his broadcasts. He has for many years vouchsafed to the atmosphere daily and has everywhere steadied his people. He has told them the truth. He has warned them. He has chided them. He has rallied them and he has given them hope. In homes all over the universe, millions have gathered faithfully around the utensil and been comforted by the wisdom of his words and the calm authority of his voice. He has spoken with quiet dignity, often in times of peril, often alone.

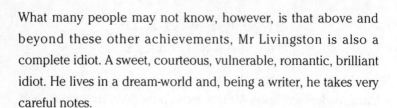

What many people may not know, however, is that above and beyond these other achievements, Mr Livingston is also a complete idiot. A sweet, courteous, vulnerable, romantic, brilliant idiot. He lives in a dream-world and, being a writer, he takes very careful notes.

# ILLUSTRATOR'S NOTE

It has been ten years since Flacco first foisted his foibles upon my hapless happenstance and I am begrudgingly grateful to this belligerent boiled egg on stilts for affording me a few pages to preserve for posterity my supplicatory scribblings to accompany this inaugural collection of Flaccophilia.

Flacco at first showed little interest in 'condemning my thoughts to the papyrus prison', until lured by a proposition from Penguin. Flacco was somewhat disappointed to find Penguin not to be of the Phillip Island variety, and is currently negotiating his next publication with a Pinnaroo Mallee Fowl.

**P. J. Livingston**
**The Fall of 1995**

# Author's Note

Greetings, Poignant Friends,

Firstly, I would like the reader to bear in mind that I am no stranger to the cloistered corridors of the literary elite. As can be attested by my well-documented association with James Joyce, which began shortly after we met in unoccupied France. I don't know if you've ever been to France when it's unoccupied, but it was a fairly lonely place with just myself and James wandering aimlessly amid the deserted cafés of the Left Bank.

Enough to drive one to distraction. And indeed Jimmy's later works bear testament to a mind with little else to occupy itself.

And I quote:

'Absinthe for me, savvy? Caramba! Have an eggnog or a prairie oyster. Got a pectoral trauma, eh, Dix? Pull the blind down, love. Got a prime pair of mincepies, no kid. O gluepot sir? Spud again the rheumatiz. Your corporosity sagaciating O.K.? How's the squaws and papooses?'

Unquote.

It's terrible when they lose it like that.

I would also like to set the record straight on rumours concerning my alleged relationship with Virginia Woolf.

It is true Virginia and I go back a long way. We never actually met as such, but we each go back a long way. Can it be just mere coincidence, or indeed fate, that drew us to live out entirely different lives?

Mind you, I did receive a spate of letters from Ms Woolf at one time, but why she constantly referred to me as Ethel Smyth I'll never know.

I would like to now share with the reader this correspondence I received from Virginia in the summer of '29.

And I quote:

Dear Ethel,

How I tremble with excitement! This day I have completed a work entitled 'The Mark On The Wall'. A tragic episode about a certain scuffmark on the skirting board. The term 'skirting board' being for me the very essence of patriarchal domination in contemporary architecture. And just why this cross-dressed shaved oak should be wearing a frock in the first place is indeed questionable. Thus confirming my suspicions about Carlos, our handyman, what with all his talk of perpendicular ballcocks and the like. Oh how I hunger for non-gender specific hardware items!

But enough of this, let's get back to me. My dear Ethel, it appears I have been misinterpreted once again. This time by the rapier tongue of E.M. Forster. It seems 'E' took umbrage to a certain paragraph ...

And I quote:

> 'The bucket was half full of rainwater, and the opal-shaped crab circled the bottom, trying with its weakly legs to climb the steep side, trying again and falling back, and trying again and again.'

Unquote.

It appears 'E' took this to be a symbolic representation of my suppressed sexuality clawing its way out of my testaceous Id. Whereas it was simply a reference to a mud crab Leonard had proudly brought home after spearing it whilst testing his tosterone at the seashore.

Ah critics, Ethel! Why do they continue to Ms Construe even my most innocent Epigrams? But now, dear one, I must away. Why oh why have I not heard from you? I receive nothing apart from some inane scribblings from a Mr Flacco of the Antipodes. Or is this just one of your little jokes, my petal?

Yours in conjectural vilification,

*Virginia Woolf*

Unquote.

And that was the last I heard from Virginia.

Let me just finally bring to your attention this blatant example of a male author's plagiarism of Virginia's work.

First, let us examine a much overlooked piece at the very beginning of *Orlando*.

And I quote:

> 'This book is sold subject to the condition that it shall not, by way of trade or otherwise, be lent, resold, hired out or otherwise circulated, without a similar condition, including this condition, being imposed on the subsequent purchaser.'

Unquote.

I personally believe this passage to be some of Virginia's most sublime work. But if I draw the reader's attention to a recent copy of Tim Winton's *Cloudstreet*, written some fifty years after Virginia Woolf's death, we find this intriguing passage.

And I quote:

> 'This book is sold subject to the condition that it shall not, by way of trade or otherwise, be lent, resold, hired out or otherwise circulated without a similar condition, including this condition, being imposed on the subsequent purchaser.'

Unquote.

Sound familiar, Mr Winton? It would seem that Master Winton is indeed Virginia Woolf in sheep's clothing!

I now urge the reader to read on with the assurance that said cerebral ramblings which follow have spilled exclusively from the percipient haemoglobin of yours truly.

**Flacco**
**Circa 1995** AD

# FUTURE TENSE

'The shallows are deep
in this moribund creek,
where the far is as
near as the here'*

*Anon*

*(Philological epigram to be printed at the beginning of chapters in the hope of
adding philosophic poignancy to what follows.)

HAT follows is this:

It is said there is no time like the present. I presume this was stated some time ago, which leads me to conclude that there was no time like the past. So to truly understand the present I believe we must study the future and learn from our impending mistakes.

A noble theory in anyone's book (and this is not just anyone's book) although once put through the rigours of empirical experiment, one continuously comes up against the vexatious problem of how to observe the future without said future collapsing into past.

I believe I have found the solution. You see, I have ascertained the

precise location of where the future lies and after facing the future, I had little trouble overpowering it as it had been taken aback by my affront, and the future is now in my hands.

And just quietly, it's not looking good, indeed it appears a tad bleak. In an attempt to consolidate the future, I employed the services of a psychiatrist, but this backfired when the doctor endeavoured to take the future back to its inception. In the ensuing confession, the future surpassed the present and inadvertently revealed the doctor's own imminent decline into insanity and a slow painful death. With that the doctor duly lost his mind and stapled himself to a rottweiler.

The tragic result is that the future is constantly dwelling on its past, i.e. the fall of Rome, the black plague and the marriage of Mr and Mrs Hitler. To further complicate matters, it has taken to the bottle and keeps me up till all hours singing 'Those Were The Days'.

The one ray of hope I have noted is that it has taken a liking to my Burmese sealpoint, Harry, whose future seems secure.

So I can only ask you all to be patient for the present and let the future take its course, and remember, let go of the past, you never know where it's been.

# LIVING IN FIN

T HE other day, rather foolishly I admit, I mistook an Anglican Church for the Post Office and, after asking the rector for the Australian bush insects and rare moss collectors' edition, I was shunted into a pew.

Might I say, I have never in my life had to endure such codswallop, the wallop of this cod was beyond belief!

You see, this chap, or chaplain as he would be known, was harping on about a tale which could only have been fabricated in the mind of one suffering profound delusions. We were asked to accept the premise that a certain Mr Jonah obtained security of tenure in the abdominal cavity of a humpback! Now, having not actually lived in many species of seafood, I still personally have grave doubts regarding the tenuous tenancy of this glorious mammal ... (Mind you, I did know a bloke who lived on yellowtail for several months but at no stage did he enter into a lease with any of these fillets.)

And when I voiced my objection to the congregation, I was promptly ejected from the premises. So I just put it all behind me as I wandered home past the burning bush, then parted the creek before foolishly taking a wrong turn at a Sodom where in hindsight I turned into a pillar of salt and was later sprinkled onto a John Dory and consumed with guilt and gluttony.

Fortunately my sole was saved for the last supper.

*No room at the aquarium*

# †HE ᴍOU†H
# ORGAᴨ

ᴍY mother used to say to me, 'Flacco, you're all ears, you've got eyes in the back of your head and your mouth is bigger than your stomach ...'

I realise now, of course, that my mother was suffering from a deep conflict of evolution. In refusing to accept the choice of natural selection, she had regressed to the inner reaches of her limbic memory.

Her mind was arrested in the time when the origins of the bodily organs were fighting for prime positions on the amorphous human form.

For example, in pre hetero erectus man, the mouth was centred in the small of the back. Of course, the small was much bigger then, so the mouth was actually located in the big of the back ...

These backbiting creatures became extinct for many reasons, not the least being severe tooth decay resulting from the inability to reach the mouth with a toothbrush. The one advantage they did

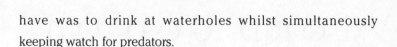

have was to drink at waterholes whilst simultaneously keeping watch for predators.

But it was the social disadvantages which eventually brought about the downfall of these exotic creatures. Take, for instance, the ancient dinner party ritual, where eye contact was kept to a minimum and most conversations centred on cave textures and hand-blown artwork.

Their culture eventually collapsed when suspicion and paranoia crippled them as they began talking about themselves behind their backs.

And so over the aeons the mouth has made its way to the privileged position it holds today, where it is free from one's foot being put in it, from placing one's money where it is, and speaking through one's millinery.

# LORD GOD ON HIGH BEAM

I N an attempt to cope with my stressful lifestyle I have taken up meditation. The ancient art of sitting on your lotus concentrating on not concentrating.

I must admit the desire for ultimate nothingness did not at first appeal to me, being myself a great fan of continued somethingness ... But after sitting for some time, unminding my own business, suddenly, nothing occurred to me. My mind drew a blank ... It was then that I realised I had reached nirvana, bliss, total enlightenment!

My entire body had transformed into a beam of light. I felt myself careering at great speed ... pure light and energy ... Suddenly, before me appeared a vision of a giant red kangaroo. It was at this point that I realised the light that I had transformed into was the high beam of a semi on the Hume Highway.

And it was here that I observed that God was in all things. For you see, almost instantaneously, the great animal had become one with the bitumen. I could no longer see where the roo ended and

the road began! Oh praise the Lord!

And I looked upon his work and lo! ... it was all over the windscreen.

# JACKANAPIAN BEANS TALK

I N my youth I was much confused by the tale of Jack and the Beanstalk. It soon appeared to me that the lessons learned in physics class would not conform to this classic tale and so I cast doubt upon the authenticity of this event in my end-of-term paper entitled 'Mechanistic Limitations of Cellular Autonoma', where I proved beyond reasonable doubt that no only did Jack fabricate this story, but the journey itself remains untenable in its intrinsic assumption of non-linear biogenetics.

Let me put my case. You see, even for Jack to climb the average shrub he would need to weigh no more than a praying mantis. Alternatively, this beanstalk must have had immense girth, as may have been the case had Jack been mistakenly given a seedling of a Canadian redwood. Still, the lad would have had to wait over one hundred years for the tree to be cloaked in even the lowest cloud cover.

Then the mighty cumulonimbus itself would not hold the weight of the boy, let alone a gigantian humanoid who had somehow developed the unlikely technique of being able to differentiate

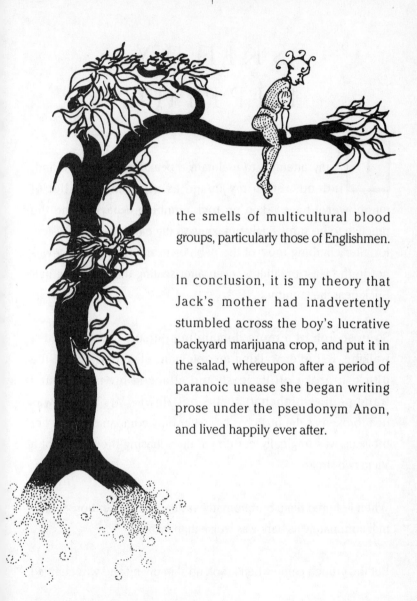

the smells of multicultural blood groups, particularly those of Englishmen.

In conclusion, it is my theory that Jack's mother had inadvertently stumbled across the boy's lucrative backyard marijuana crop, and put it in the salad, whereupon after a period of paranoic unease she began writing prose under the pseudonym Anon, and lived happily ever after.

# SKiNNY
# DiPPiNG

i N my attempts to maintain a peak level of fitness and, indeed, retain my image as a pulsating bullet of manpower, I have taken up rock climbing. I have found the practice to be surprisingly untaxing on the cardiovascular system for after climbing most of the pebbles in my rock garden I was not in the least breathless, even after scaling that daunting half brick near the laundry.

So in search of a more demanding pursuit I took up bush walking. But after walking my reluctant oleander around the block, it broke off its leash and attacked my neighbour's frangipani, which had to be put down. Mrs Lasuli was heartbroken as the bush has been her only companion since her hibiscus was tragically cut down after chasing the wheels of a Victa two-stroke.

When I offered her a bud from my azaleas she set her bonsai onto me. Fortunately its bark was worse than its bite.

But the crunch came when I took up skin diving and was charged with manslaughter after I leapt from the shed whilst attempting to dive into the skin of Mrs Lasuli, who was sunning herself on the lawn ...

It's a cruel world.

*Bark*

# THE RUDE
# AWAKENING

ANY people benefit from acquiring the skills of self defence, whereas I have taken up the much neglected art of self offence, where by constantly offending yourself you can become resistant to even the most soul-destroying insult, leaving you equipped with quite an armour with which to fend off the personal jabs of your fellow man.

For example, if you were to spend a day assailing yourself with the gibe, 'I am a moth-faced, encephaliphic mollusc whose mother was raped by a maggot-infested rock ape ...' you would find that after this exercise even the perennial, 'Why don't you lace up your mouth and rent your head out as a football' becomes a mere insignificant slight.

So in order to amass your self-offence forces, why not start now by humiliating yourself for just five minutes a day, eventually building up to a full forty-minute harangue after three months' hard slag.

You may then fancy entering the annual City To Slur, which sees thousands of punters with disparaging signs on their backs reviling themselves before a jeering crowd, whose constant heckling will leave only one remaining offender, who will receive a mooning from his opponents before accepting the catcalls of the crowd.

Positions are now available for my self-offence masterclass, incorporating the ancient secrets of tai cheek.

So book now, and you too can be a bilious bladder boil of acidulous badger's pus.

# ǐnfantasy

RECENTLY, I threw a baby out with the bathwater ... How it got in there in the first place is anybody's business. You see, my home has become infected with infants. I don't know how they're getting in.

Just this morning I caught a couple blubbering in my fruit loops and was forced to throw out the whole packet. I then lured one out of the bread bin with a rusk but it turned on me. In the struggle which ensued it would take me two hours to prise it from my nipple.

I heard a gnawing in the drawing room. After ignoring the gnawing till the early hours of morning, I followed a trail of Kimbies and found a little uncircumcised four-pounder teething on the sideboard.

When I eventually did manage to get to beddy-byes I was awoken by the patter of tiny feet, only to find myself being carried bodily to the rumpus room, where I was forced to read 'The Pobble Who Had No Toes' until they finally nodded off.

I'm at my wits' end. I've tried sprinkling infanticide around the

skirting boards – to no avail.

But if you do have this problem, whatever you do, don't become attached to them. For in no time they'll eat you out of house and home, reach adolescence, misbehave in shopping malls, disown you in public, criticise everything you hold true, leave home, bond with their analyst and accuse you of undermining their psyche, eventually leaving you to rot on the pension, finally loving you with all their heart after you're dead!

It's a cruel world.

*Madonna and child revisited*

# DEMEANING
## ⊙F LIFE

I T never ceases to amaze me how some words have managed to find their way into the dictionary. For example, how often have you been in a conversation and casually dropped the term PERSPICUOUS?

To make matters more confusing, if you look up PERSPICUOUS it means 'easily understood'.

Do we really need these unnecessary and mystifying terms in our everyday speech? I think not. It is my belief that without these superfluous words, the average dictionary need only be the size of a small pamphlet – or brochure or leaflet or handout or circular or booklet or newsletter or mailshot.

And quite often the dictionary meanings are vague and misleading. For example, I looked up the word MONGREL and found the definition to be 'Any creature resulting from the crossing of different breeds or varieties.'

Now surely we're talking BASTARD here. So I looked up

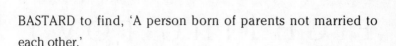

BASTARD to find, 'A person born of parents not married to each other.'

Which in no way describes the bastard down the street who ripped off my secateurs. And if you look up SECATEURS, you'll find it right next to SEBACEOUS, 'A greasy secretion of a fatty substance.' Which is a perfect definition of the mongrel who stole my scissors-like cutting instrument for pruning shrubs.

Finally, in order to find out if this book had any meaning at all, I looked up DICTIONARY and it said, 'This sure ain't no *Margaret Fulton's Cookbook* you're holding here, you little MICRONOMOUS, SATURNANIAN, PHILACTEROUS, TRUCKLEBEDDED INVIGILITE!! Look that up and you'll know what a dictionary is, son! So here's looking up you, kid.'

So I looked up YOU, which read, 'The ordinary pronoun of the second person or unspecified person or people in general.'

Hmmm, is that really me?

# FİGHTİnG FⓄWL

I AM intrigued by the depths of depravity to which the human race will plummet in its abuse of the lower order species. Take, for example, the ancient art of cockfighting, the pitiful pitting together of game fowl for pleasure and profit.

It is said the sport was popular in ancient Greece, particularly in the time of Themistocles who, whilst moving his army against the Persians, came upon a pair of fowl in full fight. He gathered his troops around them, calling attention to the valour and obstinacy of the feathered warriors, and thus his army duly slaughtered the Persian Hun.

Well, what a pity Themistocles et al did not happen upon a pair of mating spatchcocks. Perhaps now Europe would be reaping the benefits of 3000 years of Greco-Persian cross-breeding.

And recently, whilst strolling through a peat bog near my adobe hut, I myself was intrigued to come across two leeches locked in mortal combat. The furious spat ended in a draw after both engorged each other and the ensuing existential paradox caused them to question the virtue of bloodsports, with the result that

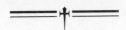

they became strict vegetarians and were promptly swallowed by a cane toad whilst feeding on plankton.

It's a cruel ecosystem ...

# IT'S A BIRD, IT'S A PLANE, IT'S SUPERNOVA

I T is a fact, my friends, that in 6 point 2 billion years our sun will explode in a monumental cosmic event known as a supernova, wherein all life as we know it shall perish. As we stare in the face of imminent catastrophe our governments should be taking steps to prepare for our untimely demise.

Yes the time is nigh! It's only 6 point 2 billion years to midnight! If you care for your future you will join me now in my proposed plan for the salvation of our race. By my calculations, if we start now, by the year 5 point 999 billion, working at a rate of 3 point 2 metres a day, we could have in place a suspension bridge spanning the length of the galaxy to the Orion nebula. Having calculated the costs of such a venture, I believe all the future motorist need to do is pay a toll of 86 point 9 billion dollars per passenger for the next 330,000 millennia, a small price for the redemption of mankind!

Unfortunately there is one drawback to this drawbridge, you see,

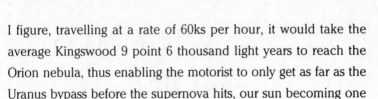

I figure, travelling at a rate of 60ks per hour, it would take the average Kingswood 9 point 6 thousand light years to reach the Orion nebula, thus enabling the motorist to only get as far as the Uranus bypass before the supernova hits, our sun becoming one hundred million times brighter than itself for several days.

To cope with this minor detail I have arranged a stopover on Neptune where you may view the destruction of the Earth through Cancer Council approved Ray-Bans of course, then continue your journey, arriving at your destination some 10 thousand light years later, with the result that upon looking back toward Earth, you may catch a glimpse of yourself packing your bags before the big event. This being the case, I urge you all to wave toward Centaurus as you pack the boot of the Kingswood, and smile to your future selves, who will be blithely videoing yourself for all eternity.

So happy motoring, and remember, if you shrink and drive, you've probably hit a black hole.

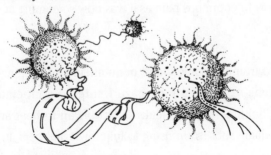

# THE CRYING GAME

MY friends, recently a mysterious occurrence occurred concurrently to my countenance. For the first time in my life, I was overcome with melancholy and suddenly, my eyes began leaking, water pouring out of them.

In panic I rushed to my local doctor. I tried to remain calm as I sat in the waiting room, but by this stage the disease had attacked my nervous system and my bottom lip had started trembling uncontrollably.

But the worst was yet to come, as to my horror a newborn child next to me began leaking around the eyes. I knew then I must have passed on the contagion. This poor hapless child was obviously in enormous pain as it was now screaming at the top of its lungs.

I rushed from the surgery and in an attempt to hide my hideous symptoms from the public gaze I entered a cinema and sat quietly holding back the leaks until I began to hear around me those telltale sobs, soon rising to fullblown blubbers. In less than

ten minutes I had infected the entire audience. I slunk out of the cinema just before Bambi stumbled over his dead mother.

Mercifully, my symptoms cleared as I left the theatre, but no sooner had my eyes dried out than the side effects began. A strange, tiny convulsion began to emerge from deep within me, bearing with it this repetitive tune: ... HIC ... HIC ... HIC.

Soon all manner of people were trying to expel this demon from my body, as I was flushed with glass after glass of water, held upside down and beaten about my back.

Fortunately this gave me such a fright that the force suddenly left me and hasn't returned since.

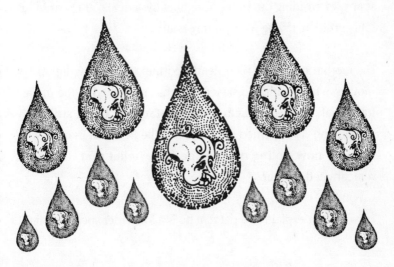

# ΠEURO⊙TiCAT

**M**Y cat is panicking. It's having its ninth life crisis. Having no innate belief in God, Oscar has become increasingly depressed about his impending non-existence. I blame myself for not instilling a sense of the divine in Oscar, but he was always a cynic, delighting in crossing people's paths on Friday the thirteenth.

Now he is constantly pawing over the scriptures to no avail, for being a cat he can't read. In an attempt to appease a notion of God he has become a vegetarian. Resulting in a glut of mice and sparrows invading our home, laughing hysterically at Oscar in his lotus position, toying with a mung bean.

His morbid obsession with death led him to recently dig up his mother, whose withered skeleton he has re-clothed in the mauve bath mat. He held a seance to contact her but a strikingly convincing vision turned out to be Rex the Pekinese in drag, who Oscar is now doting over in the false belief that Rex is his reincarnated mother.

How do you explain to a pet that he is a low-order species of little

consequence who is nought but a flyspeck on the piecrust of eternity?

Lately he had been drowning his sorrows, coming home drunk, his fur dishevelled and collar marks all over his lipstick.

It's terrible when they lose it like that ...

# H A N D B R A K E
# H I G H

Y OU will no doubt be surprised to learn that I dropped out of high school. I had no problems with the school as such, it was just the principal of the thing.

Our headmaster, Mr Calpis, was the bane of my youth. He would constantly chastise me in front of my peers, whose sneers and taunts taught me to retreat into my shell and indulge my rich and fertile inner fantasies, many involving our science teacher, Miss Billings.

But my dreams were shattered after I caught her with Mr Calpis in the storeroom conducting an intriguing experiment involving two white mice, a guinea pig, a bunsen burner, a few fatty acids and Newton's Second Law of Thermodynamics.

Later that day I was involved in an experiment of my own when a few of my classmates attempted to ascertain just how long it was humanly possible for my inverted cranium to remain immersed in a septic tank.

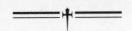

By the end of the day I was left trembling in my Bata Scouts after Ross Taflos superglued my navel to the bumper bar of his Ford Escort panel van. As he roared off into the distance, I dug in my heels and left an intricate trail of puma tracks scrawled across the burning bitumen of my motherland.

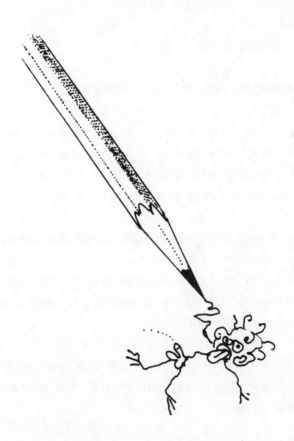

# LORD GOD ON
# HIRE PURCHASE

F EELING haunted by the past?

Racked with guilt?

Unnerved by the fragile dance of mortality?

In times of need we must all call upon a higher source, a guardian angel, an omnipotent, all-loving cosmic principal. Being myself a benevolent being of the highest order, it is with great pleasure that I now avail myself to each and every one of you.

And for a low-interest, money-back, fourteen-day free trial, you too can experience the security of unconditional forgiveness, develop an uncanny sense that all is well in this best of all possible worlds, and receive immediate confirmation that that lump in your groin is not cancer.

And, for a limited time, I will throw in unlimited access to heaven, a get-out-of-limbo-free card, plus my two-week reassurance policy.

But there's more! As an initial offer I have included the first two loads off your mind free of charge, plus an easily assemblable polished walnut shoulder to cry on.

So please send a stamped self-undressed photo of yourself to:

Redempthell Enterprises
9 Ectoplasm Crescent
Eternal Realm

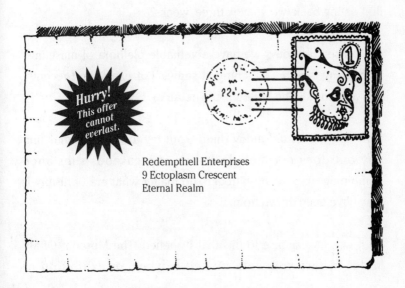

Hurry!
This offer
cannot
everlast.

Redempthell Enterprises
9 Ectoplasm Crescent
Eternal Realm

# MIND YOUR OWN BUSINESS

TECHNICALLY a museum could be defined as a public venue where humanity can view the secrets of its past and come to terms with its cultural and biological origins.

This brings me to ponder, when did the first museum appear? Perhaps an Australopithecine hunter gatherer opened the first historical museum where he presented stone axes fashioned from flint dating back two, maybe three, weeks?

Of course these days we have a veritable plethora of museums, with many curators clutching at straws. For example, I recently saw advertised 'The Museum Of The Air'.

Now call me an old fuddy duddy, but my idea of a stimulating day out does not include a tour of a gaseous substance combining oxygen and nitrogen, no matter what era of history it may have been drawn from.

So it was in response to this that I opened 'The Museum Of My Mind', where you were invited to view an exhibition of

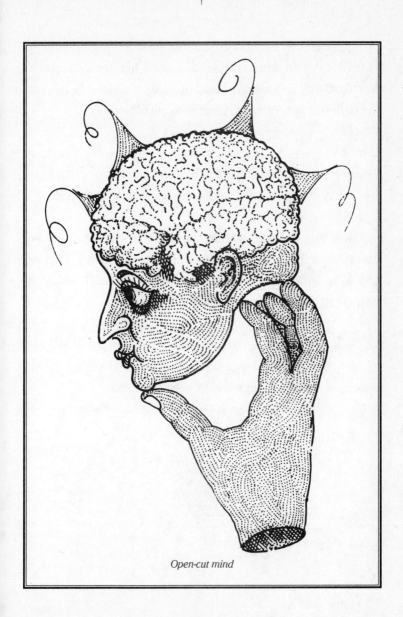

*Open-cut mind*

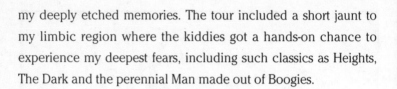

my deeply etched memories. The tour included a short jaunt to my limbic region where the kiddies got a hands-on chance to experience my deepest fears, including such classics as Heights, The Dark and the perennial Man made out of Boogies.

Then if you took a left at the biological clock, you entered my collective subconscious, and if it was feeding time you may have been lucky enough to catch a glimpse of my Hypothalamus.

My mind became a less popular attraction after I had an anxiety attack and a group of tourists were fired upon by my neurons; they were later found huddled in my cerebellum. Fortunately most escaped with only mild personality disorders.

But I was forced to close my mind after a group of schoolchildren got into my libido and experienced a fantasy involving myself, two corgis, a bicycle pump and Colleen McCullough ...

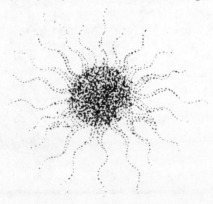

# ECİLL⊙GİCAL

S AVE the rainforests!

Protect the bilby!

Rescue the Moreton Bay fig!

But have you never asked yourselves, *'Why?'*

What has the bilby ever done for you? How often has a Moreton Bay fig sheltered you in times of financial need? Does the rainforest put a little aside each week to send your kids to college? When was the last time a humpback whale gave you a discount on a used car?

Answer me this, people! Since when has the rare and endangered flora and fauna of this wide brown land of the parched echidna ever shouted you the next beer?

Never! Nix! Nil! Zero!

Am I not correct? So why should we be expected to protect this selfish and self-supporting natural environment which cares

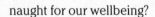

naught for our wellbeing?

How many trees have escaped conviction after murdering hapless beings who looked to them for shelter during electrical storms?

How often has the unquenchably thirsty ocean swallowed all manner of our number as they frolicked in its shores?

How many more have perished at the hands of the cruel and heartless desert?

It seems to me the environment is after our blood! Indeed, it has most of our major cities surrounded! It is we who are the endangered species!

We must act soon, before it is too late. I believe there is only one way to stem the flow of nature before it invades the very heartlands of our concrete jungles.

We must all join together and combine our skills, for it is my hope that before the year 2000 we could realise my dream of covering the entire continent in crazy paving, Australia becoming just one enormous patio, with BBQs every two hundred metres.

Oh paradise found!

# REVERSE CHARGES

'Operator! Operator! Put me in touch with my feelings.'

'Hullo? Feelings? How am I?'

'What do you mean I've never felt better?'

'Operator! Operator! Connect me to my inner self!'

'Hullo? Self ...?'

'What's the matter? Cat got my tongue?'

*'Hullo? This is me speaking.'*

'Oh what a relief. I've been trying to contact me.'

*'Yes, I've missed me too.'*

'When can I get together?'

*'I'm busy till Tuesday.'*

'What a coincidence, so am I.'

*'Have I got my number?'*

'Give me a call.'

*'I just did!'*

'Don't argue with me!'

*'I'm warning me ...'*

'Oh yeah, what am I going to do about it?'

*'O.K, O.K, I win.'*

'Nice talking with me.'

*'Oh, just one more thing ...'*

*'Hullo?, Hullo? Operator! I've been cut off in my prime...'*

# ⊤ O O ⊤ H L O O S E
# AΠD FAΠCY FREE

R ECENTLY my dentist took my tooth out. The two of them painted the town red under my very nose. I was such a fool to trust him. But he lured me into a state of somnolence before coaxing her out of my mouth with the aid of a pair of pliers.

It was obvious my molar did not at first find Dr Kolieb attractive as she resisted his initial advances. But now I'm left with a depressed gum ... you see the two had been inseparable. My tongue is numb with shock and cannot help constantly returning to the scene of the abduction.

When I confronted the dentist with these complaints, he simply replied that she was loose and it would be no trouble to replace her. He then revealed a drawer full of eligible teeth. I made it quite clear that I have never in my life had to PAY for a tooth, and none of these floosies would be welcome between my lips.

This man showed no shame, as he again delved into my mouth and probed my root canal. He then set upon my eyetooth and

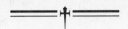

began filling her cavity! When he was finished he simply brushed her off with the rest of them ... I just don't know how I will ever recover from this violation of my ring of confidence.

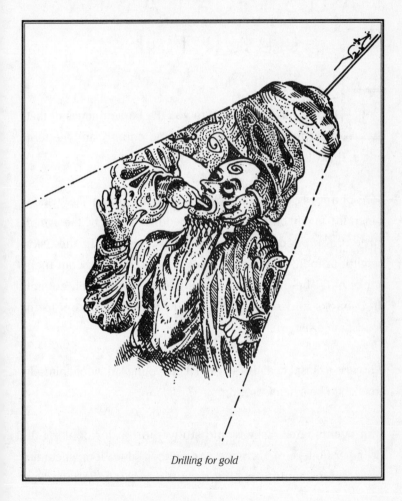

*Drilling for gold*

# GREAT MINDS OF AUSTRALASIA: PART I

I WOULD like to present to you the life and times of that great Australian philosopher and country and western singer, Dusty Esky.

Born of a lowly family of back peddlers, the young Dusty soon joined the family business and was peddling backs by the age of three. Back peddling was a lucrative business in the Esky neighbourhood, where local coal miners constantly put their backs out. The enterprising young Esky would then collect their backs and re-sell them to the hapless workers for a handsome profit.

Who was to suspect at this stage that the young lad would himself grow up to be a handsome prophet?

Some years later, Esky would study short-order cooking at Mt Buller College of Technical and Further Education, where he was to meet his future wife, but unfortunately he failed to recognise her and the marriage was never consummated. The poor woman never recovered from this oversight and the future Mrs Esky flung herself from the skirting boards of her stately home, tragically grazing her knee, leaving a grotesque scab which would stay with her for most of two weeks. When questioned about his role in this misadventure, Dusty always replied 'Wha'? Elsie who?'

It was around this time he was arrested for political agitation after throwing up on local member Damien Minton and, as fate would have it, it was to be on the hallowed walls of Pentridge the young Dusty Esky would write his first classic novel, *The Bloody Idiot*, and where he penned that immortal passage:

'I love to have a beer with Duncan,
I love to have a beer with Dunc,
I love to have a beer with Duncan,
Cause Duncan is me mate.'

Duncan has since denied any association with Esky. Indeed, he claims to be a teetotaller.

Dusty Esky died on 10 June 1896, when he was found bound and gagged, his naked body covered in yellowbox honey, a canary embedded in his urethra ... The coroner's report found there were no suspicious circumstances.

# A PENNY
# FOR YOUR
# AFTERTHOUGHTS

I HAVE been putting a little aside for my retirement.

The autumn of our life should be a time to re-live happy memories, so I have been keeping my favourite memories in cold storage.

I hope to thaw them out in my old age and, depending on how many fond thoughts I can muster in my lifetime, I intend to open a chain of superannuated markets for the elderly, where I will hire out my collection of recollections.

What joy will it be for an old timer to hobble out of my Memorable Moments Mart with a compilation of contemplations from my youth, which he can then re-live to his pacemaker's content for only three dollars nightly.

For the more frisky pensioner there will be an X-rated selection, where the age impaired will have the opportunity to share some

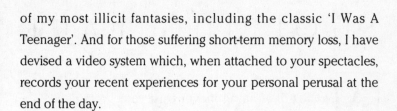

of my most illicit fantasies, including the classic 'I Was A Teenager'. And for those suffering short-term memory loss, I have devised a video system which, when attached to your spectacles, records your recent experiences for your personal perusal at the end of the day.

Imagine the delight of viewing yourself going about your daily routine, building to a climax that will have you on the edge of your dialysis machine!

For those wishing to participate in my lump sum redundancy roll over and play dead retirement fund, I have opened a chain of memory banks where you will be free to deposit your precious moments and withdraw them on retirement. This offer comes with a money-back guarantee in the event of total recall.

So Act Now! For he who hesitates ... just takes that little bit longer to get things done.

# SHOPPING MAUL

A WORD of warning: never trust your groceries. On a recent visit to the supermarket, I noticed that many of the vegetables had gone bad.

A seedy passionfruit was seen lurking suspiciously near the figs.

A carrot was arrested for indecent exposure after complaints from neighbouring dates.

A bunch of sour grapes attacked and maimed a four-year-old child and were later pureed.

A rotten tomato threw itself at a humourless unemployed actor.

A pineapple turned bad and threatened staff with its rough end.

An apple was on the turn, but found God and is currently keeping a doctor away.

The management has called for a Royal Commission into aubergines found hung in custard.

Fred Nile has questioned the relationship of two peas in a pod.

Terrorist activity was suspected when a punnet of strawberries went off in a bin outside the store.

On my way home, I was arrested when police went through my bags and found my zucchini had gone to pot and later that night, a bad egg put me in hospital.

*Completely rooted*

# †HE MUFFE†
# CONSPIRACY

I SUSPECT my mother was a perpetrator of infant cerebral sabotage. She would constantly confront me with strange tales which, in hindsight, I can only assume were aimed at paralysing my fragile eggshell mind.

For example, she would speak to me of a certain 'Little Miss Muffet', of whom I have no recollection. This alleged Ms Muffet sat upon a 'tuffet', an intriguing term whose meaning eludes me to this day. Apparently, when this unknown, unmarried young woman sat upon this mysterious concept, she proceeded to feast on her 'curds and whey'!

And whilst sitting on this unidentified object hoeing into an unknown substance, suddenly, down came a spider and sat down beside her, presumably on its own little tuffet, and proceeded to terrorise the unfortunate lass, forcing her to flee and abandon the tuffet she so loved.

As I wrestled with this complex melodrama, my mother confounded the issue by embarking on a tale about one

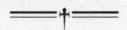

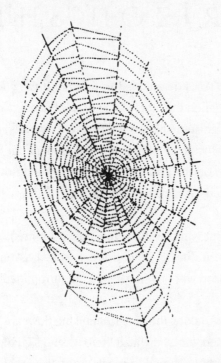

Old Mother Hubbard, who went to the cupboard to fetch her poor dog a bone ... Now, why she went to the cupboard and not the fridge is beyond me. No wonder the poor mongrel starved to death!

But when she started harping on about three little pigs settling down in a triple-fronted brick veneer home, well, I huffed and puffed and I blew her cover and had her committed.

# H·O·R·Í·Z·O·N SHÍNE

RECENTLY I determined to find out if the grass was truly greener on the other side. For this I needed, of course, to get to the other side. This would involve, obviously, crossing the horizon. A feat which had thus far eluded me. I put this down to sheer laziness on my part for the horizon could not be that far. After all, I could see it from where I stood.

So I set off. But whilst walking towards it, I turned, and noticed another horizon directly behind me. I looked askance ... It was true! The horizon was onto me. It had me surrounded!

I played it cool, taking the time to smell the flowers ... Fortunately my bluff worked, for by nightfall there was no sign of the horizon. During the night I planned to sneak up on it, so that when dawn broke I would be on the horizon before it knew.

I trod softly through the night and before long it was the darkest hour before the dawn. I knew I must be close. I felt around for the horizon, very carefully, for I did not wish to wake it ...

But it was here that my plan fell apart, for I had not considered the horizon's reaction to waking and finding a being upon its

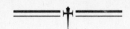

back. What if it balked and I fell off? And plummeted down the other side? What if it was not greener there? What if it was some appalling shade of puce and I couldn't get back?

There was only one answer. I had to slaughter the horizon in its slumber. So just before the dawn, I took a shot in the dark ... But I must have missed it! For when the sun rose the horizon had made its way once more into the distance.

But it appears I have made a tragic mistake. For, judging by the crimson lake spilling out across the horizon, I fear I have shot the sun!

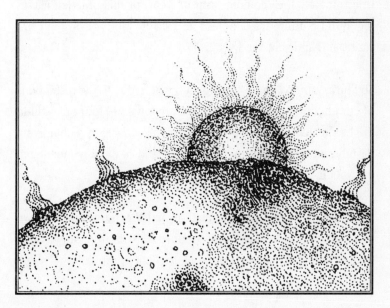

# †HE ȷOY ⊙F SL⊙†H

**M**Y car broke down the other day. It just started blubbering and whimpering that it could not go on like this. I tried to comfort it by taking the scenic route but we hit an embankment and now it's a nervous wreck.

So I have taken to cycling as my preferred form of transport. Unfortunately the required fashion wear for this practice leaves much to be desired, as I do not necessarily look my best in lycra shorts and amusing headgear.

So I have joined a nude cycling club where due to the restrictions of current human decency laws, we are forced to tour only within the bounds of each others' lounge rooms, where we gather every month and rally round the telly, at the end of the day meeting at the couch.

Obviously this has definite limitations in the fitness area. Thus we have all become obese nude people poised atop our bicycle frames, which tremble beneath our collective girth.

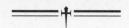

In light of this, I have developed an ingenious method of weight loss, where we attach the spare tyre from our stomachs to our cycles, then hire our bikes out to the fit and youthful who then work off our spare tyres whilst we enjoy the benefits of a day in front of the telly.

We call this program The Tour De Friggin' Nowhere ... It's a great start if you have to eat and rummage around the house all day.

*A race against time*

# HAND HELD
# HOSTAGE

S TILL waiting for your ship to come in?

Acquiring that nest egg is never easy.

So why not hold yourself hostage for an obscene amount of cash?

It is important to plan carefully from the start. You must take care not to be spotted abducting yourself. So follow your movements closely for at least a week before choosing the moment you least suspect to surprise yourself.

I chose a dawn raid after I noted that it was my wont to rise just before dawn and follow nature's call, which I answered into a small pot plant by the bed.

I saw this as a vulnerable moment and one fateful morning caught myself midstream, and before I knew what was happening I had bundled myself into the boot and sped off to a destination unknown.

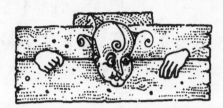

I arrived under cover of darkness. I pulled my jumper over my face and led myself into a small room where I bound and gagged myself before tying me to a bed.

I sweated it out. The standoff was unbearable as negotiations ground to a halt. I videoed myself talking calmly to quell suspicions of foul play, but secretly tortured myself in the cold light of day. I started to panic when I began refusing food. I talked back to myself and called my bluff.

Then one night, after I had fallen asleep, I slipped out of my shackles and stole into the night.

And when I got home I heard that the police were closing in on my kidnapper. I heard a knock at the door. I felt the cold steel of the handcuffs. A siren disappeared into the distance.

And that was the last I saw of me.

# THE STRANGE
# BEDFELLOW

T has not gone unnoticed, the curious behaviour of my new tenant. For example, he woke up this morning, then stood under some water for several minutes before pushing a small brush back and forth between his lips until he began frothing at the mouth and had to spit it out.

And on entering the kitchen, he proceeded to cook some water, then added some small dry leaves and a white substance taken from the udder of a cow.

He immediately began browsing through some white pages with black marks throughout, remarking that this practice kept him in touch with the entire world. Then after wrapping himself in a variety of coloured rags, he slipped his feet into what could only be described as some cattle moulded into the shape of his foot.

I didn't see him until later that night, when I caught him sitting in front of a small black box of flickering light. He stared for hours at this light, occasionally breaking into an infectious giggle until suddenly he made his way to the bedroom, where he shed his

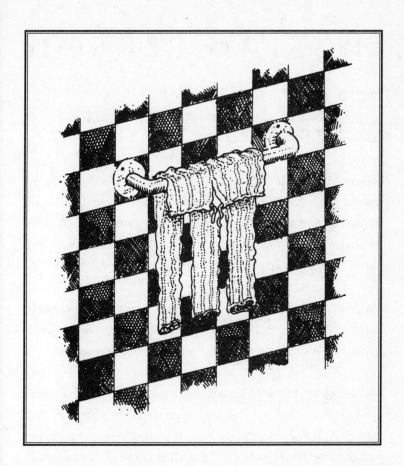

rags then lay prostrate on a tangled web of iron thinly disguised by some flattened cotton, and within no time appeared to fall into some kind of trance which lasted till dawn, whereupon I evicted him, stating we did not accept that kind of behaviour here ... Oh why do I get all the weirdos?

# mISSInG PERS⊙n

I WOKE up the other morning only to find that I'd put my neck out.

I could hear it scratching at the door. I tried to call out to it but I'd lost my voice ... it had eloped after finding that it loved the sound of itself. I tried to sit up but my back was gone. By midday my eyes were peeled, my lips were sealed and my ears were pricked. I waited, with bait all over my breath.

Suddenly, my skin crawled ... then made its way to the closet to join my skeleton. I called after my cowardly flesh, 'Show a bit of backbone, you invertebrate!', immediately venting my spleen.

My heart sank. I was on my last legs ... prompting me to wonder, just how many pairs of legs are we allocated in a lifetime? And how do you know which are your last ones? Assuming you get two or three sets in your life, I think I'm laughing, for as far as I know I've still got my baby legs ...

Eventually, night fell, causing me to wink forty times. In the morning I woke up to my self, released my bowel and let my mind wander. So now I just sit around waiting for inspiration. It is

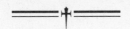

said you can wait for inspiration till the cows come home ... Just what is it about procrastination that attracts beef?

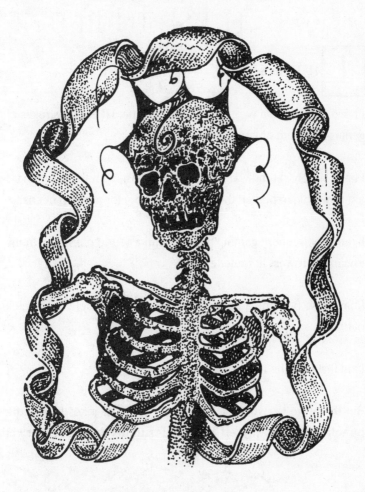

*I've got you under my skin*

# A HEAD
# OF HIS TIME

I HAVE done it!

I have conceived a way to make my fortune. Like most strokes of genius it is quite obvious once you think of it.

I have simply set my watch two minutes fast, with the result that I am now able to pervert the course of history for my own needs.

I can now frequent gaming parlours and astound patrons with my uncanny prowess at roulette.

I have also become a national hero by saving people in the nick of time.

I am first with the news, all day, every day.

But there are drawbacks, of course. I laugh at jokes before the punchline. I find myself running for trains that have not yet

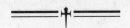

arrived at the station. I walk past maternity wards shouting 'It's a boy!', much to the chagrin of all concerned.

Recently, while driving, I skidded to a halt and had to wait two minutes for a child to run out in front of me.

But worse still I'm writing this idea before I've thought of it and it will probably occur to me right about n~ I have done it!

I have conceived a way to make my fortune. Like most strokes of genius it is quite obvious once you think of it.

I have simply set my watch two minutes fast, with the result that I am now able to pervert the course of history for my own needs.

I can now frequent gaming parlours and astound patrons with my uncanny prowess at roulette.

I have also become a national hero by saving people in the nick of time.

I am first with the news, all day, every day.

But there are drawbacks, of course. I laugh at jokes before the punchline. I find myself running for trains that have not yet arrived at the station. I walk past maternity wards shouting 'It's a boy!', much to the chagrin of all concerned.

Recently, while driving, I skidded to a halt and had to wait two minutes for a child to run out in front of me.

But worse still I'm writing this idea before I've thought of it and it will probably occur to me right about n~ I have done it!

# PUMPING
# IRONY

THE quest for the body beautiful, or in my case, the body adequate.

I believe these universal cravings for a superior anatomic configuration can be traced back to our childhood. I myself was most impressed with the Marvel superhero The Incredible Hulk. The closest I ever got to emulating this ideal was by marinating my body in GI lime, but my resulting green epidermis fooled no one and made me the butt of numerous playground taunts.

By the dawn of adolescence I believed I had found some hope for my bruised but budding masculine ego whilst delving into my father's collection of *Pix*, *People* and *Post* magazines, where an ad on the back pages featured one Mr Charles Atlas, whose generous proportions we were told could be ours in a matter of days with the aid of the appropriate apparatus, available on a seven-day money-back guarantee if not completely satisfied.

So after diligently saving my pocket money (involving going six weeks without cobbers and green frogs) I still found I could only

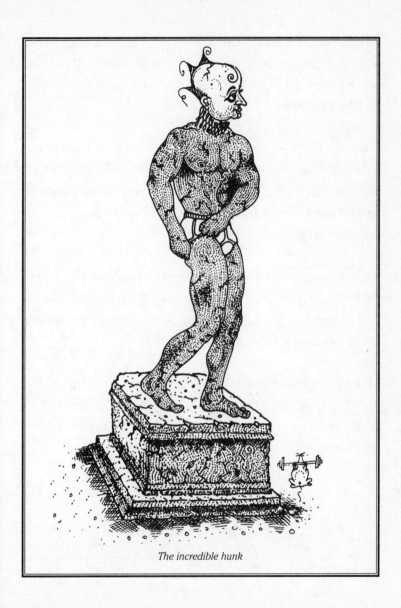

*The incredible hunk*

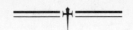

afford a small part of Mr Atlas's offer, with the result that I ended up with a rather marvellously proportioned left calf muscle, which caused me to walk with a limp and never really impressed Jennifer Peasley.

It is only with the benefit of hindsight that I have realised the futility of these endeavours. For example, we would all be familiar with the classic image of the ninety-pound weakling having sand kicked in his face by a steroid-enhanced Cro-magnon girl magnet.

A much simpler way to avoid this scenario would be to not go to the beach at all. At least not the particular beach where that big bloke hangs out, and sunbathe only on the concrete promenade where he will probably just stub his toe.

At the end of the day it is of the utmost importance to have a realistic appraisal of one's own body image. After all, any magazine that would have me as a centrefold is not the kind of rag I'd want to be reading.

# mY mOTHER's TONGUE

THERE is no doubt, that my mother was a genius. She would say to me, 'Flacco, Rome was not built in a day.' I did some quick mental calculations and found this deduction to be precise to the very second. As a matter of fact, it may have taken several days, even weeks, to complete it.

Mama would also say, 'I didn't come down in the last shower, you know.' On pondering this I soon realised my mother was absolutely spot on. For I had had the last shower, and down in it my mother certainly did not come.

*Tongue in cheek*

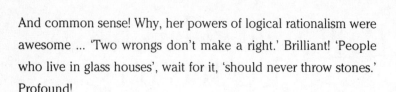

And common sense! Why, her powers of logical rationalism were awesome ... 'Two wrongs don't make a right.' Brilliant! 'People who live in glass houses', wait for it, 'should never throw stones.' Profound!

But like most great minds, the burden of her genius gradually overwhelmed her. I first became suspicious when one day she exclaimed ... 'The proof of the pudding is in the eating!' Deeply perplexed, that night I stole into the kitchen and searched the pudding, but alas, I found no proof!

And when I awoke that morning, Mama was going on about a horse refusing to drink some water it had been led to and something about unhatched chickens remaining unaccountable.

Mama spent her last years in a futile search for a peck of pickled peppers picked by Peter Piper. For, according to Mama, if Mr Piper did pick a peck of pickled peppers, then does this peck actually exist, or is it just a nexus created in the mind to organise the input of experience so as to preserve the coherence of the subjective realm and allow the body self to function in a purposeful way?

Alas my friends, we will never know. For not long after this, Mama was taken away when she decided that I was the salt of the Earth, and attempted to sprinkle me over the bratwurst ...

# HAROLD THE DAUNTLESS

THIS is the story of Harold The Dauntless, whose life was plagued by daunt.

At dawn the daunt began when Harold would be challenged by his cat, Inglasious, whose habit it was to disturb Harold's slumber

with a sandpaper tongue to the testy. Undaunted, Harold one day solved this perplexing predicament by slicing Inglasious's salacious tongue with a Stanley knife, leaving the tongueless Inglasious to slowly go insane trying in vain to lick the wound.

But it was the morning shower ritual which daunted Harold, whose custom it was to wash himself thoroughly before showering in an effort to save precious water, but what truly daunted Harold was the fact that, owing to limited space in his modest studio apartment, the shower recess was situated on the balcony, where on windy days Harold's vinyl Rubens nude print shower curtain would ride up his body, eventually revealing to the neighbourhood Harold's startling genitalia, an unwelcome sight at the best of times, and 6 a.m. was definitely not the best of times. 6:45 a.m. was the best of times, when Harold would have finally managed to extricate himself from the shower curtain and the taunts of the local school children, to whom Harold had become the butt of their jokes with their jokes of his butt.

Not to be daunted Harold eventually managed to save face (among other things) by showering in the flush of his toilet bowl. This not only cleansed the dauntless Harold but expelled him to a sewerage outlet only metres from the bus stop, where Harold the dauntless would don his jacket. Thus Harold, and his jacket named Don, dwelled dauntlessly on ...

# CUTE
# TICKLES

I HAVE developed the rather unnerving habit of biting other people's nails.

This can prove somewhat embarrassing, as was the case when a young woman sat next to me on the tram, her long, fine cuticled, highly enamelled digits entwined alluringly before her. I managed to contain myself for three stops before suddenly burying my face in her lap and in no time had lustily gnawed her nails to the quick.

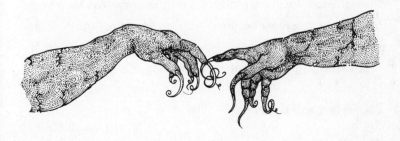

I must voice my protest at the treatment I suffered after this unfortunate event, when I was promptly ejected from the tram in no uncertain manner. Surely I cannot bear total responsibility for

my actions? I mean to say, this woman must have known what she was doing as she trimmed and filed her nails into those gentle, come-hither curves, with just a hint of half moons peeping through the pale pink enamel which had been brushed up and down each finger, up then down until they bore a sheen no hot-blooded nailophile could possibly resist!

My life has been ruined, as I have now stooped so low as to only find gratification by engorging myself on offcuts supplied to me by my local manicurist.

Society is to blame. Why cannot we take a lesson from the Moslem cultures, where women are forced to wear black thimbles in public?

Unfortunately, I feel my problem is getting worse, as I have lately become increasingly besotted with my toenails. And with the long summer months ahead, how am I to survive those winsome G strings of the pavement, the rubber thong ...

Oh, get thee to a pedicurist!

# BEEF SHORT CUTS

**M**Y father was a cruel man, frequently offering advice which was obviously meant to confound me. He would

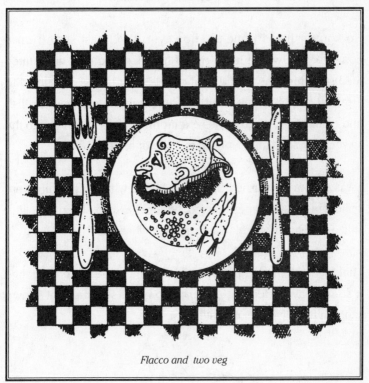

*Flacco and two veg*

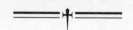

say, 'Flacco, you've got to take the bull by the horns ...' Well, needless to say I still bear the scars.

It was effort enough just finding a bull in the first place, let alone securing its cartilaged antlers, but I finally unearthed a prime beast at the rear of the local abattoirs. To my relief the animal had recently been slaughtered, making for a relatively simple opportunity to grip its pointy protrusions.

No sooner had I done so, however, the beast set off on a conveyer belt where in no time I had been skinned and gutted then sold through various local outlets where I was consumed to a mixed response, my father devouring my forelock with relish and calling for seconds. The next morning I was excreted into the sewerage system and expelled into the open seas.

I was eventually washed up onto a beach where my family were holidaying. My father exclaimed, 'Where have you been, you little shit!' while my brother kicked sand in my faeces.

That night my mother put a nappy on me but then had to change it straight away, leaving me in my present state, a faint brown stain on the tile grout of existence ...

# LORD GOD ON HIGH HEELS

I HAVE uncovered the very fabric of the universe.

It appears to be a kind of gingham tweed with a cross cable stitch. Believe me, it comes up beautifully against a black meaningless void, which reminds me, those black holes need darning ...

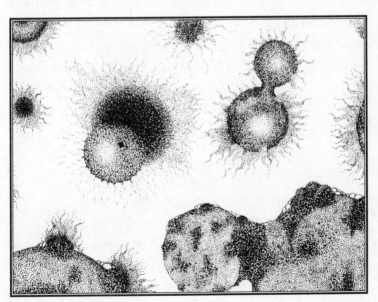

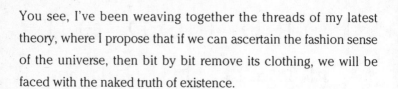

You see, I've been weaving together the threads of my latest theory, where I propose that if we can ascertain the fashion sense of the universe, then bit by bit remove its clothing, we will be faced with the naked truth of existence.

I have discovered the strange material surrounding the constellation Centaurus to be of mauve-sequinned lurex, whose orbit I have observed traces the shape of a rather comely negligee.

Our own Milky Way itself appears to form an immense feather boa, and the halo of gas surrounding the Orion nebula is composed entirely of talcum powder. When we ask who could have possibly created such a cosmos, we are faced with the unthinkable prospect that God may in fact be a screaming queen!

And the fact that the universe is expanding is a sure sign that she is not in the least concerned about keeping her weightlessness down.

So in an attempt to contact our maker, I have taken up drag racing in the hope that pitting myself against cross-dressing Maoris in tutus and fishnets will bring me closer to God, our Father, who art in Heaven, Carlotta be thy name ...

# PIG
# PENNIES

I FEEL we must be especially sensitive in the ways we instruct our young. My mother often complained that our house was not big enough to swing a cat in, and to this day I am perplexed as to why she spanked me when I proved this not to be the case, except in the bathroom, where Tibbles met his untimely end ...

*Boaring 747*

Also, I was severely scolded when on discovering my mother carried a rabbit's foot for good luck, I attempted to boost her chances by replacing it with the fetlock of Phar Lap.

On my fourth birthday my mother gave me a piggy bank, which was to have dire consequences in later years, as I was seriously injured at the zoo when I attempted to place my penny in the back of a feral warthog.

I have since decided against placing your savings in any member of the animal kingdom. For one time, when I did manage to force over three hundred pounds into the gullet of a Gosford pelican, it flew south for the winter, staying at only the best motels and living it up at my expense.

My mother also expressed the intriguing proposal that pigs might fly, and even though I seriously doubted the outcome, having secured a baby hog, I flung it from the roof of the shed, whereupon, despite its best attempts, it failed to catch even the slightest updraft.

So believe me, if you're thinking of living high on the hog, forget it, there's no money in it anyway ...

# A FETE WORSE
# THAN DEATH

I N the face of a crumbling patriarchy and being an unsensitive old age guy, I have taken it upon myself to form my own anti-men's-group men's group, M.O.N.G.R.E.L. (Men Offended by New age Goody goody Ratbag Effeminate Losers).

Yes comrades,
    Women may have suffrage,
    But we have the bar fridge!

At our inaugural meeting we were addressed by our Patriarch, Mr Sogeny, who spoke before us, resplendent in his flowing 'State of Origin' quilt, his bare beer belly coyly hiding his manhood and from behind just a hint of cleavage peeping alluringly atop his long stubbies.

A highlight of the day was Mr Sogeny's revelation of the ancient men's mysteries, including such contentious issues as 'Which Australian batsman scored consecutive ducks on the '62–'63 Ashes tour?'

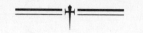

Following this was a host of activities including a stall where the mystic, King Wally Lewis, read our football cards. The great meat debate raged on for hours, 'Beef Short Cuts? Not the Full Feed!'

After the 'Reclaim The Weekends' march, as the sun set, we gathered around the bonding barbie, upon which we sacrificed a couple of S.N.A.G.s ... The screaming wimps did not go down too well, too tender.

After this there was a touching moment when we observed two minutes' silence to hear Ken Callender's memorable call of Race Four from Randwick, Rex Mossop's Handicap.

We drank from the keg of plenty, which was followed by the obligatory cleansing chunder ritual. We then formed a circle and took turns mooning the moon (and believe me by this stage it was not only the moon that was full).

We ended the night arm in arm, in deference to the Great God 'Makita', the still, cool air being cut only by the chanting of our sacred code of ethics,

'Here we go,

Here we go,

Here we go.'

Add nauseum and you have a top night out.

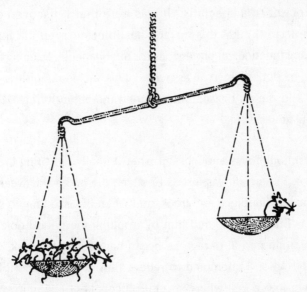

# LAW AND
# DISORDER

THE other day I visited my doctor complaining of chest pains. He's always complaining of something. I also suspect him of being a thief, for the last time I saw him he took

my pulse. When I asked him for it he said it was normal. Well it may be normal for him, by now he probably has pulses coming out of his ears!

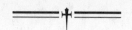

I had long suspected that this doctor was somewhat perverted, and my suspicions were confirmed when he requested I remove my shirt, poke out my tongue and urinate into a small jar. When I inquired whether it was his practice to ask this of all his patients, he readily supplied the damning evidence that he did this tawdry ritual several times a day and to women and children as well!

I decided to expose this poor demented being before he could wreak any further damage on the community so I took my complaint to a specialist. It was here that I discovered the horrible truth, that this malady has infected even the highest ranks of the medical profession. For after patiently listening to my story, he put me on to an associate of his, a cold, inquisitive chap who laid me on his sofa and queried the nature of my deepest sexual fantasies.

Well, enough was enough! But when I finally did bring them to justice, I knew all was lost as I noticed the judge was wearing a suspicious hairpiece and frock, and when he asked me to swear on his Bible I humoured him by insulting the good book for a while, until in a fit of rage he began hammering his desk with a mallet! When I attempted to relieve him of this weapon, I was thrown into a cell where several officers kept taking down my details ...

Is there no end to this depravity?

---†---

# †HE S†ORY ⊙F HAPPY CLEⲘ

J OVIAL, jocular, happy, happy Clem.
Roars of laughter, at the barber, in the K-Mart,
At the dentist, happy, happy Clem.

Life of the party, M.C. for all occasions,
Happy, happy Clem.

Look! Look! Kiddies ... it's Clem! Happy, happy Clem.
(And who bounced the kiddies on his knee at Christmas?)
Happy, happy, Clem.

........................

This is the story of happy Clem.

Roly poly, chub chuckle, happy, happy Clem.
Big red nose Clem. Bounce belly bald bawdy Clem.
Roguish raconteur, happy, happy Clem.
Risque, ribald Clem.

Large heart, hearty laugh, likes a flutter,
Happy Clem.
In a swimsuit, varicose vanity, hairy backed,
Happy Clem.

Big bum, bung leg, breathless asthmatic,
Happy Clem.

Pock ridden, thyroid troubled, gout inflamed,
Happy Clem.

Unmarried, tiny dicked, fat ankled,
Happy Clem.

Lone living, one-room flatted, rat infested,
Happy Clem.

Illiterate, underachieved, unremarkable, pencil-chewing,
Happy, happy Clem.

Stiff, bloated, two-day-old,
Choked on a cream bun,
Happy, happy Clem.

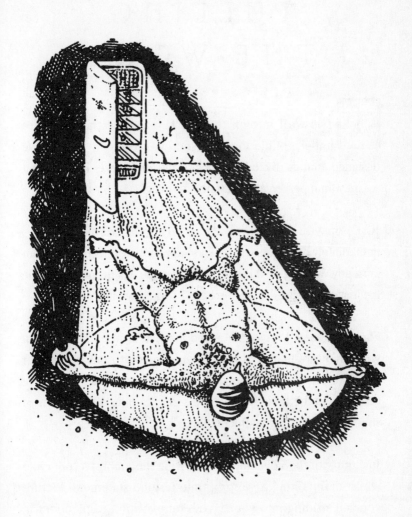

*Clem ... 4 a.m.*

# PULLING
# THE WOOL

I T is well known that all sub-atomic particles are imperceptible to the naked eye. To rectify this, I have designed a range of clothing specifically for the eyes in order that we may then perceive the essence of being.

Just pop your eyes into a pair of my Harris tweeds and immediately tiny spots will begin to appear before your eyes. I am currently working on a three piece pinstripe which should enable the iris to perceive the double helix of your own DNA.

For sports fans, I have conceived a range of pupil pullovers in your favourite team colours, to enable you to grasp the finer points of the game. And my swimwear designs make it possible for a day at the beach to include some startling observations of subcutaneous quantum fluctuation.

Just think of the advantages of viewing the anthropic principle whilst maintaining an appropriate fashion statement! Picture yourself striding into your favourite nightspot, resplendent in Armani optic overalls. You spot a gorgeous manifestation of

random perturbations at the bar and join them in a dry neutrino ...
And before you know it, you are the toast of the Mandelbrot Set!

*This has been brought to you by 'Quantum Peep', makers of fine ocular eyewear.*

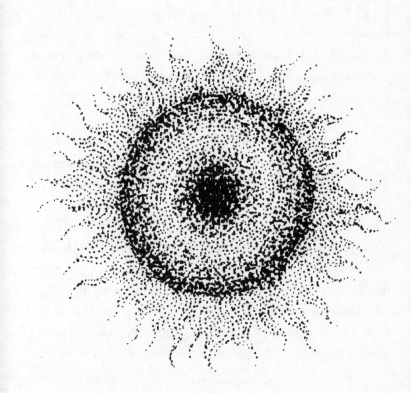

# A WORD IN THE HAND

**M**Y friends, I'm at a loss for words.

I searched my vocabulary but the only words I could find were FLUMMOX, SCROTUM and PAPOOSE. Words for which I have no possible use.

If only I could find a word like LEPIDOPTERA, which could be useful for all manner of things, especially if I were an order of insect with four wings covered in gossamer scales ... Unfortunately I am not of this species so the word has failed me.

But thankfully I always keep my word. So I have retained the term SYLLOGISM, a form of logical reasoning consisting of two premises and a conclusion, which only brings me to the conclusion that I must choose my words more carefully and thus avoid situations as when I once chose the word PHENOBARBITONE, and fell asleep upon the instant.

In my youth my father gave me his word, which went straight over my head. And when I asked Papa the meaning of the word, he laughed maniacally and sang, 'We'll build a word of our own that no one else can spell ...' So I am now the proud inheritor of the term XLOXOCLOZIZ-PVERN-PVERN ... Eventually I did discover its meaning, which was on the tip of my tongue, but unfortunately I was mugged by a man who took the words right out of my mouth.

Mind you, I still have the last word ...

ZYGOTE

# H⊙m⊙
# AUSTRALiS

C AMPING has long been a popular lifestyle in this country and whilst researching this phenomenon under the shade of a coolabah tree, I couldn't help but notice a suspicious character stuffing a rather jolly jumbuck in his tuckerbag when up jumped three uniformed troopers with gay abandon and asked for the next waltz.

I soon discovered that Australia's cultural gender imbalance goes much deeper than this when I encountered a wolf in sheep's clothing, which led me to ponder the extent of crossdressing in the monotremata of this wide brown land.

I determined to expose this mammalian masquerade and within no time I had unearthed some mutton dressed as lamb, and I immediately smelt a rat. The rat smelt of bourbon and had a sheepish grin. But the cat was out of the bag when I opened a can of worms after following a big bad wolf to a low rent dive where I found it under the covers in a low-cut teddy mumbling, 'All the better to eat you with, my dear.'

I left with a nasty taste in my mouth and as I made my way back I was propositioned by a dingo in a matinee jacket and was almost trampled by a herd of wildebeest in beehives singing downtown.

And when I arrived home, a bearded dragon came out of the closet wearing a mink stole and snakeskin boots, which shed themselves to reveal a naked mole rat on ecstasy. Although this rare species is protected in wilderness areas like Darlinghurst, Tasmania has mounted a campaign against them.

Mind you, that's about the only thing that gets mounted down there these days ...

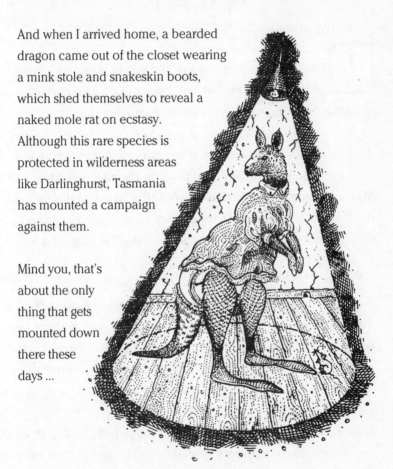

*Skippy, queen of the desert*

# CLUE CLUCKS CLAN

**T**RAGEDY has plagued my family, its sabreous scythe whittling away my lineage. You could say I was the last in a long line ... but now I'm the first in a short line.

As a child I had so much wax in my ears my father threaded a wick through my head and stood me on the table to illuminate his clandestine dinners with my Aunt Millie, who herself suffered from a rare skin condition where her pores were unnaturally large. Indeed her pores were on average the size of a five cent piece.

For a time I wondered what Papa saw in her, but soon realised there was barely anything you could not see in her. Perhaps he was attracted by the play of light on her thinly veiled exoskeleton, or was it that alluring hint of bladder lolling provocatively over her belt?

Papa himself was afflicted with perennial dandruff, making us all very wary of his one culinary specialty, the lamington. My mother never cottoned onto Papa's flirtatious rendezvous with Millie, due

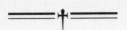

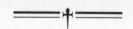

to an annoying complaint that runs in the family. Her perpetual diarrhoea kept her in the bathroom for twenty-nine years.

Unfortunately tragedy struck our family after a complication involving my Grandpa's ingrown toenail, which grew through his foot and into the lino, eventually wending its way to the rumpus room where it strangled my four-day-old nephew before impaling the canary.

But the shit really hit the fan when Uncle Remo's colostomy bag was caught in the rotor of my Airfix World War I Sopwith Camel. Soon after this my cousin, Strange Robert, took to the family tree with a chainsaw, leaving me an orphan. The orphan died and left me a small nest egg which I sat upon for months in the hope of hatching offspring and was soon the proud father of four.

This numeral grew to become a complex number who went forth and multiplied, with the result that I have become the goose that laid the Golden Mean ... Serves me right for putting a square root in a round hyperbola.

# THE
# EPECLECTIC

I T is time to release Art from the bondage of gallery walls and place it into the hands of the masses. To this end I intend to follow in the footprints of that great liberator of Art, Mr Lazlo Toth, who, as you know, took to Michelangelo's Pietà with a clawhammer. An action which was widely misinterpreted. For it was Mr Toth's intention to chop the Pietà  into thousands of pieces, each which could be sold for a fraction of the cost of the original, thus placing the great master's work into the hands of the very people it was intended for!

The same could be done with the statue of David, which could be ground down to a fine powder and sprinkled around the homes of even the most poverty-stricken art lover.

But why stop at the visual arts? What about poetry? Why not sell Walt Whitman by the word?  Surely a Whitman 'and' would be within the reach of most budgets?

I myself have bought up as many words from the great poets as I could afford and find myself the proud owner of this remarkable piece.

## I SING THE BODY ELECTRIC JUG

Shall I compare thee to a burning deck,
For the word had passed about that Mary
Had a little frog he would a wooing go
Ride a cock horse.

I love a sunburnt captains
And the kings depart 'twas brillig
And the slithy toves do not
Go gentle into that good diddle diddle.

**by George Bernard Kipling**

# ·OF MEN AND MICE

I|T seemed my father had difficulty distinguishing between certain mammalian species, for he would say to

*Sir Lancalittle*

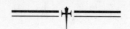

me 'What are you son, a man or a mouse?' To me the solution was obvious, but to pacify Papa and avoid further confusion I would always make sure I walked exclusively on my hind legs, avoided squeaking as much as is humanly possible and would rarely scuttle along the skirting boards in the dead of night.

Unfortunately one morning, after hearing me rustling through the newspaper, my father set a trap for me and I would have surely perished if Papa had not freed me after noticing a family similarity around the lumbar region.

So in the face of this my father sent me off to the army to make a man of me. The armed forces attempted to complete this alchemical gender experiment by forcing me to sleep with fifty other men, share the same showers and occasionally slaughter the odd fellow man.

Unfortunately I was dishonourably discharged after honourably discharging my rifle whilst protecting my honour against my commanding officer who commanded the tenth commandment after mistaking me for his coveted neighbour's third wife.

My father never lived this down, but I said, 'Cheer up, Pops, after all, life's not all beer and skittles.' With that he sank a tinnie and hit me with a nine pin ... It's a cruel world.

# invest in
# PEACE

I HELD a seance recently to try to contact my late cousin Milo who still owes me twelve bucks for re-tiling his patio.

And as we held hands around the table, our medium began speaking in tongues. At first I was disconcerted and presumed that our medium was perhaps well done. But soon the dulcet tones of cousin Milo emerged from within the happy medium. Milo was well pleased with himself for an extra twelve bucks can

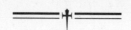

go a long way in the hereafter where it has long been the case that you can't take it with you.

But Milo had pulled a swifty, and instead of entering the gates of heaven Milo did a deal with Satan, whereupon old Beelzebub sold his soul to Milo for twelve bucks. The Prince of Darkness was grateful for the sale as the bottom had dropped out of the used soul market, what with the resurgence of atheism and eastern religion in the post-Christian society.

From then on it was a simple case of if the soul fits wear it. And wear it he did, for now Milo has become the successor to the Devil and has set himself up in the subterranean burbs of lower east Hades, where he has bought a lovely asbestos residence, beautiful brimstone fireplace, delightful earthly garden ... The only drawback is the agonising screams from the neighbours burning off for all eternity. But Milo calls it home.

So my only recourse to recovering my money was to sell my soul to the ex-captain of the damned, who snapped up the offer, with the result that I am now the anti-Christ and am so doomed to roam this earthly plane for all eternity, suffering itchy lice and dreadful tinea. Still, I figure I'm twelve bucks up on the deal and when I do finally shuffle off this immortal coil, well, with friends in low places, I know cousin Milo will never let me down ...

# ΠOΠ
# EXCiSTERΠCE

Y OU will be pleased to know that I recently survived a sixteen-hour overnight rail journey across this wide brown land of insistent dirt.

Why is it that my ticket always seems to include: a breathless asthmatic, a schizophrenic Paraguayan with halitosis, eight-day-

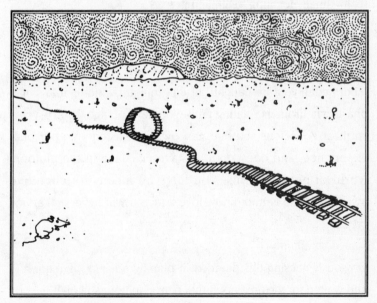

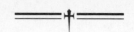

old quads and a man who thinks paediatrics to be of great interest to the entire carriage?

At three a.m. nature called and after navigating my way to the rear of the carriage, I entered the water closet, both water and closet being the operative words ...

I secured myself within this sacred cubicle and, after finding my sea legs, took aim and hoped for the best. On completion of this feat without hitting my feet, I searched high and low for the button that would expel my corporeal evidence to the outer realm, finally locating a sign which read:

TO FLUSH,

DEPRESS FOOT PEDAL

Well, who am I to argue? I crouched down and whispered to it, 'Foot pedal, you are naught but an armature winding in a single phase synchronous rotating field. You have no ego, soul, psyche, spirit or conscious self that can owe its existence to personal experience, and consequently have no place in the plutonic world of natural forms. You have no means for cognitive awareness, you cannot know love and you will never lick an ice cream ...'

Obviously sensing this paradox, it blankly refused my request ... and waited for the next nocturnal patron to pour shit on it.

# UΠSHELLFÍSH
# BEHAVÍOUR

S O tell me, my friends, why is it that the human species is so infatuated with frolicking on the beach?

Whilst observing this phenomenon recently, I was amazed at the spectacle before me. Scantily clad humans toasting themselves upon white dirt.

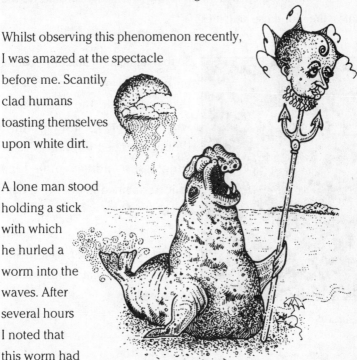

A lone man stood holding a stick with which he hurled a worm into the waves. After several hours I noted that this worm had

*Seal of disapproval*

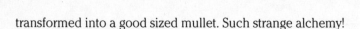

transformed into a good sized mullet. Such strange alchemy!

The more sunconscious of these creatures wore suits of rubber, and not content that this was protection enough, they spent most of the afternoon deep below the surface of the ocean.

Paradoxically, it was only when the sun went down that these creatures made their way home. Now surely night would be the safest time for these activities?

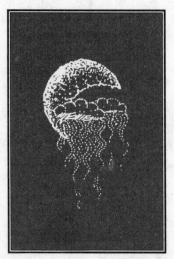

So that night, after liberally coating my body with minus 15 moonblock, I stole down to the beach and, while undeniably a little chilly, I found no need for umbrellas or sunglasses and my pine lime splice remained intact for several hours.

But unfortunately I was killed when a stray manatee mistook me for some kelp ...

# WAKE IN FRIGHT

THIS morning my dog brought me my pipe and slippers. This confused me as I do not smoke and would not be seen dead in a pair of olive corduroy slip ons.

The plot thickened when my son Ezekiel asked my permission to leave the table. Having never married, let alone borne offspring, I was somewhat nonplussed by these occurrences. It was obvious this was to be a day unlike any other.

It was only later, as I sat in my office overlooking a vast Nordic landscape, it dawned on me that during the previous night I had inadvertently slipped into a parallel universe where I had become the King of Norway.

I decided to make the most of my twenty-four hours. I quickly invaded Sweden and after occupying Denmark I declared war on Switzerland. Unfortunately I fell asleep before taking Belgium.

Meanwhile in my own universe the King of Norway had awoken in a two-bit bed-sit in Woolloomooloo and, after calling for his pipe and slippers, was met by my Aunt Cynthia sucking on a White Ox, with her cross kelpie, Eric, humping the royal knee.

They immediately fell in love and I was shocked to wake up the next morning handcuffed to my bed, my Aunt Cynthia's wispy beard gently tickling my Campari-soaked tutu.

The King of Norway awoke to a world in crisis, and was soon overthrown by an angry mob after refusing to instigate my proposed legislation to outlaw mime, puppetry and the poetry of John Laws.

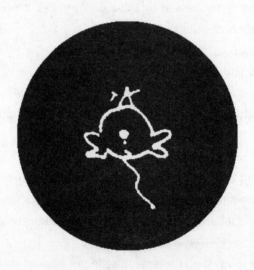

*Beyond the black (mouse) hole*

# STARK RAVING MUD

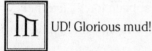UD! Glorious mud!

A sublimely phonetically apt term, don't you think? After all, what is mud, but mud?

What is the meaning of mud?

Just look around you at the influence mud has had on our society. Our culture is built on mud, from the humble adobe hut to the towering infernal skyscrapers. Indeed, we spend our entire lives frolicking on this beautiful revolving orb of mud.

And in the beginning, life itself was originally drawn from the primordial slime. (Yet another fancy term for mud.) What simpler recipe for this womb of life? Take some dirt ... and wet it!

But slowly, through the eons, mud has become a dirty word. For example, if one is deemed irresponsible, it is said your name is mud. If one casts malicious slurs, one is labelled a mudslinger.

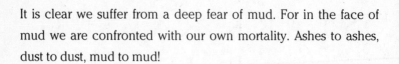

It is clear we suffer from a deep fear of mud. For in the face of mud we are confronted with our own mortality. Ashes to ashes, dust to dust, mud to mud!

Mud is the beginning and the end, the alpha and the omega, but through our fear and ignorance mud has been forced into hiding, only venturing out on rainy days, when you may find it huddling in the crevices of your boots.

Most of today's mud has been driven offshore, as is evidenced by the fact that the bottom of all our great oceans are covered with it!

Has it never seemed mysterious to you that somehow the mud ends precisely on the shoreline? Why does not the mud make its way up the beach to our doorsteps?

Because it knows it is not welcome! Indeed it is scraped from the feet on that most mud-ist of inventions, the welcome mat!

So I urge you all to slip, slop and slap on a mud pack.

And may the filth be with you.

# FİJİ OR NOT FİJİ

I WAS disturbed to hear the other day that man is not an island.

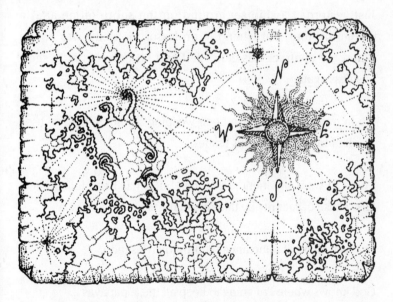

This came as a great shock to me for I have lived the past eighteen years under the delusion that I was a small atoll just north of the Galapagos Islands.

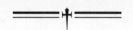

The Galapagos Islands themselves will be shocked to hear that they are in fact the Brewster family holidaying in the Pacific basin.

This news has been disastrous to my native inhabitants who have established a remarkable culture which is about to collapse under the weight of my realisation that I can't swim.

Just yesterday a ship set ground on the shore of me after a three-hour tour, but when the professor realised I was not an island my contract was cancelled and I'll never work in show business again.

I'm in quite a state. I have been weeping so much that I've used up all of my subcutaneous tissues.

I tried to warn my friend Tasmania, but it has been lulled into a false sense of security by thinking that it is part of Australia.

So it is with great reluctance I return to civilisation.

God knows where I'm going to keep all these papayas ...

# LET THERE BE
# A LIGHTER

W HAT is this insignificant bulb of soil we call our home but a grain of sand in the endless desert of the cosmos, and we are but moist shell-less molluscs bathing in the shallows of perception.

Yes! These are the BIG questions! But then, what about the little questions? Surely as insignificant bubbles of breath in a boundless continuum, we have much more in common with the tiny issues?

Take for example, the seemingly innocuous contemplation, 'Hmm, I wonder if I left the gas on?'

Well, if one hasn't, then all is well in this best of all possible worlds ... But imagine a universe in which the gas IS left on! And in this lethal void, it would take but one humble homo sapien to strike the first match and lo! the entire solar system would explode in a massive chain reaction, sending whole galaxies spinning out of control, imploding and expanding throughout the illusion of time.

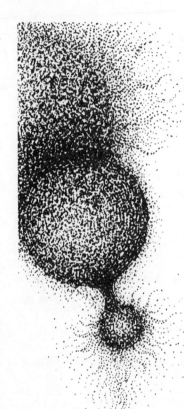

Sound familiar? Of course! For it was just such an insignificant event that brought our own universe into existence. You see, in the beginning, God ducked out for a smoko, and the Lord spake, 'You wouldn't have a light on you, would you mate?'

And behold, there was a light ...

Which brings us to the obvious conclusion, that in a non-smoking cosmic environment, there would have been no chance for our species to have evolved!

So I therefore believe all cigarette packets should bear this message:
'WARNING – SMOKING MAY CAUSE THE QUANTUM EVENT FOR THE CREATION OF FREE-THINKING SENTIENT BEINGS'.

It is said that God does not play dice ... but he does get through two packs a day.

# †HE FAX

## ⊙F LÎFE

### AN OPEN LETTER TO GOD

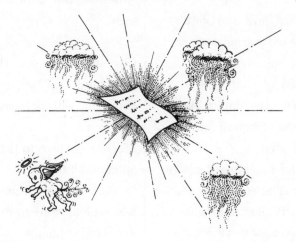

D | EAR Almighty Creator of Perpetual Munificence.

How goes it, omnipotent one?

Having recently read your engaging collection of short stories, I was hoping you might make some time (as indeed is your wont) to respond to my humble queries.

Firstly

Does the epistle of the apostle
Of St Peter at the altar
Alter Paul's apocalyptic
Episodic paradigm,
Involving David and Goliath
Whose old testament relyeth
On the strength of Moses'
   tablets
And a brightly burning bush.
And was it that your son
   had farted
That the waters dear departed
Or the fallacies of Pharisees
Whose Phallocentric fantasies
Have paraphrased the epithet
Believe to which we are
   thus led
That catechisms of Cathology
Whose entepistemology
Declares quite categorically –
I have on good authority,
The immaculate conception –
That your son was born a lamb!

Also, if I could bring to your
attention a certain typographical
error I noted whilst perusing
your parables. My copy reads:

'Honour your Lord God on
high'.

Obviously you meant, 'Honour
your Lord God "up" high'. I
hate to be pedantic, sorry.

PS Give my love to the Holy
Spirit and if he happens to be
in the area, tell him he is
welcome anytime to drop by
and dwell within me.

Amen.

# LİFE CYCLİNG

A TIME IN MARCH,
THE MARCH OF TIME ...

I N my youth I was sitting in a park, watching a dog foolishly barking up the wrong tree, just generally minding my own business, having a ponder, a bit of a think, just

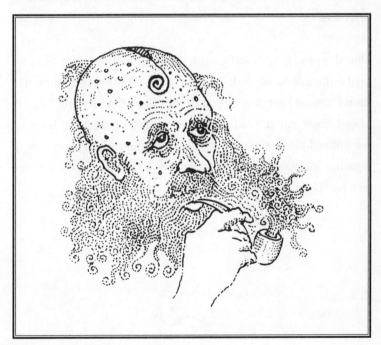

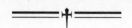

sitting there, cogitating, and next to me was an old cogertating.

He was nearing the end of his days. Fortunately he had amassed a large backlog of nights which he planned to survive on for several years. He had kept these dark hours well hidden until they were cruelly stolen by a thief of the night.

Now he spends his days running from the dawn, trying to gain more hours by outrunning the sunset, this resulting in him continually circumnavigating the globe, maintaining a mean time of 11.53 a.m.

One day, as he sprinted across the international date line, he broke the speed of dark and had a near-birth experience. He found himself speeding through a dark tunnel, a blinding light lay ahead. Suddenly the old man gave birth to himself and he lived his entire life over again, eventually finding himself on a park bench ... cogitating ... next to him was a young cogertating. Just as it had been all those years ago ...

# EARTH
# BOUND

**I** DO like to be beside the seaside.

But in fact, the side of the sea is a side of the sea which has eluded me.

You see, I have never managed to tilt the ocean on its edge to get a peek at its side. So I just content myself with watching the rocks pounding against the surf and the shore

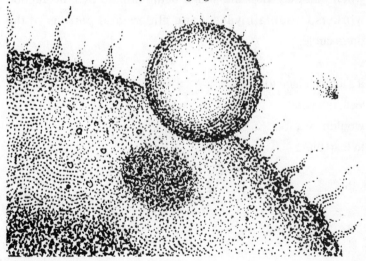

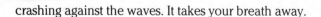

crashing against the waves. It takes your breath away.

Which causes me to ponder, have you ever considered the consequences of a world in which humans did not exhale? Over a period of time the Earth would become a vacuum, trod by red-faced beings who asphyxiate in less than three minutes!

Such is the fragile balance of our biosphere. So breathe easy my friends, and be thankful you do not inhabit a little known planet just east of Epsilon, where the sky ends just three point two metres from the planet's crust.

The tragic plight of its people can be observed on a clear day when one may view the planet being orbited by construction workers, mountain yaks, hang gliders and patrons of the dress circle.

It's a nice place to visit, but you wouldn't want to leap there.

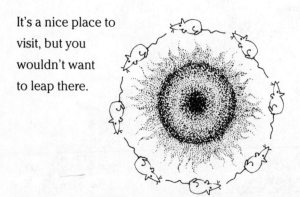

# ME AND MY
# BIG IDEAS

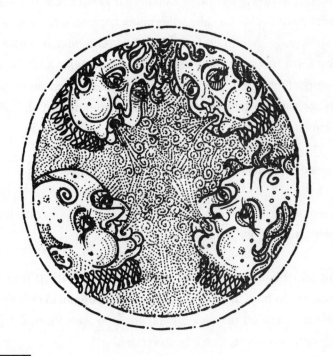

W HILST sitting in my bath, legs akimbo, as is my wont, taking the time to pause and reflect my cause and effect through all of time's Sundays ... a thought crossed my mind, hung a left at my thorax and circumnavigated my cranium before

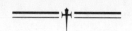

emerging from me in what lesser humans may interpret as a sneeze.

Never underestimate a sneeze, for the much maligned sneeze is actually the violent release of a massive buildup of creative ideas which have decided to abort the miserable soul who refuses to acknowledge them. Left to roam outside the human soulcase, they form feral packs of unique ideas, wreaking havoc on unsuspecting simple folk, who may find themselves sitting at a bus stop when they are suddenly overwhelmed by the urge to scream,

'Eureka! Every action has an equal and opposite reaction!'

So remember, my friends, when you last sneezed, you may have ejected the cure for lymphatic warts ...

And so, this one awesome sneeze expelled itself like an abomination from the very nostrils of God. It trembled in front of me, this pompous unnerving idea, arms on metaphorical hips, tapping its existential foot. It bellowed forth:

'Behold! Diamonds are forever! But oranges are for half time ...'

# †HE FREAK
# ⊙F ΠA†URE

W HERE do you draw the line between freakdom and normality?

For example, all manner of limps, lumps, lank lobes, not to mention lisps, are generally considered within the norm, whereas a lopsided lesbian with a harelip and a townhouse in Hobart would be considered a dead set freak!

But let's look at the grey area between the conventional and the curious. For instance, take the accepted behaviour of your average household pet ... A prime example would be my Burmese sealpoint, Harry, whose dextrous skills never cease to amaze ... yet draw not a raised eyebrow from even my most highbrow house guest. Whereas if 'I' were to squat on my coccyx and commence to lick my genitalia on the shagpile, I would no doubt be labelled a freak, albeit a rather envied one ...

But indeed the most bizarre of behaviour goes without the bat of an eyelid in this stranger than fictional family of man ... Look at our worship of sporting heroes. We adore that person who can hurl themselves over a stick just that little bit higher than anyone else, or who can ride their bicycle in continuous circles just a little faster than their fellow man.

The ideal of masculinity is the chap who has gained the lumpiest body through constantly picking up heavy things then putting them down again for several hours a day. These people are our cultural yardsticks, role models for our youth, yet some families will still hide their freakish relatives from the public gaze.

Take for example that great traditional Australian cricketing family, the four Chappell brothers: Ian, Greg, Trevor and Sistine ... Yes, the little known Sistine Chappell who bore a remarkable resemblance to a Renaissance cathedral. Needless to say Sistine showed scant talent for cricket and has been kept hidden beneath scaffolding for most of his life. This genetic glitch on the Chappell dynasty can be traced back to their distant forefather, Medici Chappell, who in a fit of obscure lust married a Florentine Piazza.

All this brings to light the tragedy of Trevor Chappell's controversial underarm bowling incident against New Zealand in the World Series. The sad truth is that Trevor was terrified of bowling overarm, for in so doing would risk revealing his armpit, and the flying buttress therein.

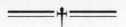

Trevor now lives in disgrace, and has long since gone into hiding inside his brother. So be kind to architraves, especially if they're looking a little under construction.

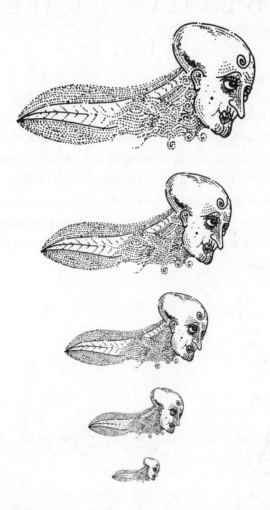

# iT's nOT EASY BEiNG TRUE BLUE

I T is my belief that you can take environmental consciousness just that little too far ... For example, in the face of the continuing destruction of our rainforest, one activist recently chained himself to a Tasmanian oak. Unfortunately he was felled with the great tree when his protest went unnoticed as his regulation jungle-green overalls successfully camouflaged him against the sub-tropical landscape, his screams unheard above the chainsaws.

To add insult to injury, he was turned into paper pulp and ended up as a minor article on speculative market capitalisation on the Dow Jones Slump.

And furthermore, why do these people call themselves greenies? Is not nature blessed with the full spectrum of hues? Should not then an ecologist working specifically in the area of offshore pollution be called an aquamarinie? Or a campaigner for unleaded paving paint a mission brownie? Whereas a tireless worker for more tasteful bathroom decor would be known as a duck egg bluey.

Mind you, these pinko lefties pale into insignificance when faced with the black and white reality of a greying Australia, as these white collar blue rinsos hold the balance of power with the redneck majority in this wide brown land of the blue-arsed fly.

# †HE İGL⊙⊙ H∧S L∧U∏DERED

I RECENTLY attempted the first nude crossing of Antarctica. Unfortunately I came unstuck when my mother, not comprehending the point of the exercise, headed me off at the first kilometre, urging me to take a warm pullover.

Noticing my lack of loin covering, she screamed, trying to protect the family jewels with the pullover. I flung it asunder and jogged into the distance, leaving her sobbing in the sleet and snow.

I never saw my mother again. Legend has it she froze in the ice and was eventually licked back to life by a passing polar bear.

The story goes that Mama settled down with the bear and lived happily for many years. The bear eventually became easy prey for predators due to its roaming the snowplains in a fair isle sweater. Mama would not let him out without it.

It is said she was worshipped by the clan, who became distinct for their fashionable snow wear. But my mother inadvertently became the cause of these bears' extinction. For you see she

*Pierre's cardigan*

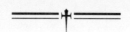

insisted on keeping them out at night, and night being six months long they perished, scratching at the igloo.

After many aborted attempts, I eventually succeeded in my nude crossing, but alas was thwarted by cruel fate for I arrived at the South Pole only to find the entire Prime Minister's IX mooning the aurora australis.

Although there is some contention among the team that they may have been pipped at the pole by a sighting of Mama heading north with a bear behind.

But when David Boon insisted the bear was wearing a maroon polo neck skivvy, they decided to keep the whole thing quiet or risk losing our finest silly point.

All this is true, I swear it, as God is Mike Whitney!

# †HE VOⓈCE ⦿F DⒾSAPPROVAL

MY voice spilled across the yawning ravine, but still my echo refused to speak to me. It had become fed up with its hollow existence, doomed to roam misty valleys, dark tunnels and rat-infested wells.

It threatened to come out of the cavern and lead a life of its own, fulfilling its dream of becoming a baritone like its late father (who worked for Mario Lanza).

I was wrought with angst ... This echo knew me only too well, and could be a liability. The last thing I needed was another mouth to feed.

I turned to leave when suddenly my shadow crept up behind me and pushed me over the brink. As I lay at the bottom of the abyss, I heard my echo bounce around the cavernous walls, mocking me in the voice of Mario Lanza.

And together they lived out the rest of my life ... just a shadow and my former self.

# ΠΕΧΤ YEAR'S
# ΠΟDEL

I RECENTLY attended the premiere of an Andy Warhol retrospective in the year 2067, where there has been a revival of 20th Century Pop Art.

In a remarkable feat of Post-Post Modernist eclectic genius, the artists of the future have succeeded in cloning Andy Warhol from a single hair follicle taken from his blond wig, which has been enshrined at the Guggenheim.

The Warhol clone, excited by the marketability of himself, is said to have immediately set about cloning a limited edition of 2000 Andys which have been immediately snapped up by the local illuminarty-farty. For having an original Warhol in your home has become the very height of 21st Century chic, the art elite rubbing shoulders with their own Warhol whilst perusing the New York club scene of the 1960s via their Virtual Reality berets.

Unfortunately the Warhol clones have become something of a liability, as their constant bitching with each other has had them banned from many of the exclusive Art Pods.

Not to mention the copyright problems that have emerged as a result of the clones churning out endless prints of soup cans and hundred-year-old celebrities, which have flooded the market, with each clone claiming original ownership.

But by far the biggest sensation of 21st Century art has surfaced in that cultural Mecca of the future, Deniliquin, where art historians have discovered the work of Pro Hart. This has been hailed as the greatest find since the unearthing of those timeless works by the late 20th Century master, Rolf Harris, with Hart's works fetching exorbitant sums at the current exhibition now being staged at the Ken Done Institute.

Unfortunately Harris's work has suffered a decline in popularity of late since he was cloned and Deniliquin has been swamped by marauding hoards of wobble boarding Harrises wreaking havoc on the arts community.

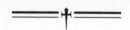

But the single greatest controversy came after the cloning of Jackson Pollock, when the clone broke down and admitted that all his works were executed by his cocker spaniel, Avril, whom Jackson would spray with gouache, then lock in a shed walled with primed canvas, allowing the dog to shake herself clean before repeating the procedure with another colour.

Avril has since been cloned, and has herself now become the most prolific painter of the new millennium, doing a roaring trade with her latest print series of Pal Meaty Bite cans, much to the chagrin of the Warhols, who of late have been gunning each other down in their lofts with the result they have become a dying art and their prices have skyrocketed.

So my advice to those artists of the last decade of the 20th Century who are seeking immortality through their work, why not follow the example set by Vincent Van Gogh and sever a lump of your own DNA, then encase it in perspex and call it Portrait Of The Artist As A Crypto-Graphic, Dia-Critical, Homo-Analogical, Proxemic Kenisis Of A Trappist Monk; by the time they've deciphered the title, you'll be rubbing shoulders with Warhols, Harts, Harrises and a spaniel named Avril.

# LET THERE
# BE DARK

I N the beginning ... night fell ...
No day ...
     No dawn ...
       No dusk ...

Meanwhile the universe expanded, wearing itself so thin in some areas that other universes began to appear, manifesting themselves as tiny beads of light, peppering the endless night.

Far below, in the nether here nor there regions, the appearance of these new universes fell on deaf eyes, for these tiny netherbeings had but four senses – taste, touch, smell and sound – but unfortunately neither of the two senses which distinguish they from we, i.e. sight and common.

It was during this endless night that a child was born unto two of these beings. A beautiful bouncing baby boy ... Two arms, two legs, two ears and unbeknown to either Shirley or Jack, there, resting beside the bridge of his nose, their son sported a pair of moist pale orbs.

'Let's call him Ngorrbshtruxingghh,' said Jack.

'Sounds good,' replied Shirl, 'We'll call him Ng for short.'

As Ng grew, it became increasingly obvious to himself and no one else that the two blue spheres occupying his countenance (which his parents took for gaping boils that never seemed to heal no matter what manner of ointment they applied) were unique to him and him only.

For most of his life these lumps lay dormant, useless against the black void that surrounded him, until once in that long night, as he walked along the seashore, staring as only he could at the sound of the crashing waves, slowly, imperceptibly, a dim light appeared ...

He stood transfixed, as the light grew greater. What was this? Suddenly it dawned on him ...

For the first time, Ng looked around him at the futility of these wide-eared creatures who plod that particular planet. For a time he delighted in running naked through the townships, pulling faces and making rude gestures at those in positions of authority. What a card!

So it came to pass that Ng, because of his persistence in his bizarre theories of light, colour, form and fire (and a failed business venture involving glass-bottomed boats) became increasingly ostracised and isolated by his fellows, ending his days in confusion, losing his marble, placing all his eggs in the same basket, the square on his hypotenuse being nowhere near the sum of the squares on his other two sides, and eventually starved to death whilst busking as a mime ...

It's a cruel space time continuum ...

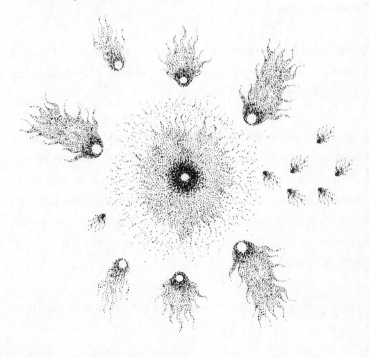

# NERVOUS
# RECKONING

I AM witness to a recent event which drew little interest from the media. Thus I feel it is my duty to bring to the public's attention the second coming of Jesus Christ, which occurred just ten days ago in an isolated area due north of Coonabarrabran.

It was quite a spectacle. Fire, brimstone, all manner of manna from the heavens. But the only gnashing of teeth of note was from a dozen heifers grazing nearby.

It seems Mr Christ and his entourage of immortal souls made a wrong turn at limbo, with the result that our Lord and saviour was forced to hitchhike some twenty kilometres to a nearby town, where he announced his return to the patrons of the Conargo Arms Hotel. He was met at first with contemptuous mirth, followed by cold stares, and finally the almighty left hook of Gibbo the publican.

Normally the Lord would have smote the town with pustulant

scabs, but unfortunately he had left his smotes in the glovebox of his winged chariot.

For the past week the Son Of Man has been staying at my place where he has become increasingly depressed, as his attempts to gain media access have drawn only one response – from a local newspaper which featured the Almighty in their 'Seen Around Town' pages. The Redeemer of Humanity was photographed at Les Girls tripping the light fantastic with two altered boys after partaking in one too many glasses of his own blood.

The Messiah was later seen two hundred metres offshore where he had inadvertently wandered whilst trying to hail a donkey, and was fatally rammed by a jetski.

Three days later the Lamb of God appeared to a group of schoolchildren in the washrooms of Leeton Primary School screaming, 'I have come! I have come!' He was duly arrested and charged with indecent assault.

When Jesus described himself on a police statement thus:

| | |
|---|---|
| Name | J.H. Christ |
| Date of Birth | 1/1/1 |
| Occupation | Cabinet maker |
| Address | c/o Promised Lane, Hereafter |

he was forced to undergo a psychiatric examination, which concluded that Jesus was suffering delusions of grandeur and was thrown in a ward with Moses, the Pope and Napoleon Bonaparte.

As Moses read his tablets the Pontiff leaned across and asked the Lord for forgiveness, to which Jesus laid his hand upon the Pope twenty-four times with some force, until he was restrained by doctors and placed in a ward with nineteen other Christs.

Thinking on his feet Jesus promptly turned the warder into wine and fled the country after hijacking a Qantas 747 and demanding that it lead him not into Toowoomba, but deliver him from Essendon.

The headlines the next day read:

## JESUS PUNCHES PILOT
## WHILST DESCENDING INTO HEATHERTON

Is nothing sacred any more?

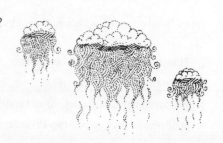

# †HE URBAN WORRiER

G US moved in mysterious ways. This drew strange looks from tourists and endless ridicule from the thoughtless natives at whose dinner parties a seat for Gus was perennially absent. This, coupled with the taunts of their cruel and heartless offspring, forced Gus into a life of semi-immobility in his modest bed-sit, where he would sit in fear of standing, for a bed-stand was four dollars extra.

As he sat in his sit, lowering his opinion of himself, listening to the sound of opportunity not knocking, he became aware of a faint glow emanating from the toaster. Gus shifted uneasily as the glow bathed his sit. After ten minutes the urge to stand overwhelmed him. But Gus held his ground, after all, to stand would mean certain poverty.

Six days Gus sat sitting, when suddenly, just as mysteriously as it came, the glow extinguished ...

In the hours that followed, Gus felt the chilly air on his skin, as he shivered beneath hospital green sheets. He had become quite

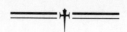

attached to the toaster this past week and was fretting its closeness and warmth, its patience, its unqualified acceptance. He longed for its return. He tried averting his eyes from it in fear that his constant gaze might be inducing its reticence. He paid far too much attention to the kettle in the hope that jealousy might entice the toaster into life.

Eventually Gus felt himself dozing off, but shook off the impulse for fear of complicating his fragile reality. For in a recent attempt to improve the quality of his existence by fitting more into his allotted twenty-four hour cycle, Gus had begun a program of waking one half-hour earlier every morning, with the result that after a month he was waking up before he went to sleep. And after suffering profound sleep deprivation, he reversed the program and has not woken since.

From this Gus has concluded that his present condition must be a dream from which he cannot escape. In his last attempt, he decided to fall asleep in this current dream, but having achieved this, he dreamt that he woke up, and is now living out that dream.

. . . . . . . . . . . . . . . . . . . . . . .

Gus turned his back and began anew his quest to count the lines cast by the shadow of the venetian blind. His present record was seventeen, but as Gus approached this elusive goal he felt a familiar warmth upon his back. He spun round and was met by the tangerine glow of the toaster illuminating the sit, as he sat, squatting, squinting into its radiance.

Gus had never felt such joy. He even forgot the time his landlord, Nodrog H'taobe, boarded up the linen closet where it was Gus's wont to sit and peer into his sit through the crack in the door, envisaging himself as a lowly pauper who might one day gain access to the palatial premises upon which he peeped. Whereupon Gus would burst into his sit and feel for a fleeting moment the aura of one who had vanquished the demons of dolorous want.

Gus could not at first cope with this feeling of imminent joie de vivre, as it slowly came to dawn upon his sombre brow, the ungodly realisation that he had no worries ... This worried him ... He immediately began searching for a problem.

He wondered if he had left the gas on ... He hadn't.

He searched the pillow for dandruff ... There was none.

He checked to see if his hair was thinning ... It wasn't!

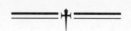

Suddenly the machine gave a shudder and in a flash gave Gus this day his daily bread, as a slice of charred black toast leapt from the toaster into Gus's waiting hands.

.......................

Six months Gus sat sitting. Six months of burnt toast forming a charcoal mound engulfing the sit, shifting every so often as another piece of toast was ejected deep beneath the pile.

Gus stared into the blackness, following the path of a lone ant almost reaching the peak before another tremor sent the tiny beast plummeting into a dark crevasse. Gus remained unmoved. He had witnessed countless cockroaches, silverfish and woodworm meet their untimely ends attempting to scale this evergrowing peak, only to be thwarted within millipedes of the dark summit.

Gus had looked forward to this day for some time, having laid a little wager with himself after calculating that today the toast would pass his navel, and indeed, as night fell, he knew he would never again see this tiny chasm of umbilical union.

And that night Gus fell again into shallow slumber and dreamt a dream he had dreamt the night before.

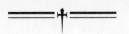

. . . . . . . . . . . . . . . . . . . . . . .

Gus's head sat neatly atop the charcoal mountain. He was gladdened by the fact that he could no longer see the shadow of the venetian, and felt reassured by the intermittent murmur of the toaster beneath him ...

Three weeks later Gus saw his last sunset ...

And from within his blackened womb he heard the voice of Nodrog H'taobe and the sounds of hammer and nail surround the sit ... Then silence ...

And here Gus sat sitting, waiting, until finally, mercifully, death put him out of his mystery ...

. . . . . . . . . . . . . . . . . . . . . . .

Postscript

Two years later ...

Nodrog H'taobe paces his luxuriant bed-stand, a warm glow emanating from his toaster ...

# THE
# PLAYS

**THE PLAYS**

i.

**WAITING FOR GODOT**

(Abridged)

ii.

**FOR THE TERM OF HIS UNNATURAL LIFE**

*OR*

**THE TAMING OF THE SCREW**

a tragedy in four acts

# Author's Note

In my day of hay as a living playwright of legendary stature, I completed the two major works reproduced herein.

These were executed around the time I first met William Shakespeare in Strathfield upon Avalon, where I walked into a bar, and the bard was at the bar, but the barman refused to serve the bard, the bastard barred the bard!

And verily spake the bard, 'Thou dare despose me? Thou that art polluted with your lusts, stained by the guiltless blood of innocents, corrupt and tainted with a thousand vices, and why? Because you want the grace that others have? No! Misconceived!'

In an attempt to defuse the situation I whispered to the Shake, 'Sire, me thinketh you drinketh enough.'

The well-oiled wordsmith then placed his velvet hand about my codpiece and spake in hushed tones, 'Your eyes are lodestones, and your tongues sweet air, more tuneable than lark to shepherd's ear.'

Methought this a somewhat brazen move.

'Sirrah' I said, 'steppeth outside where I shall anoint thy brow with forehead!'

He fixed a reddened eye upon me and said, 'Thou darest mock me? Thou that hath been hitteth with the ugliest of sticks!'

It was at this point that the bard verily projectile vomited amid my vexed persona, and fell to his knees retching dryly from his umbilicus.

Later, when he came to in the men's room, he was heard to mutter into his reflection, 'Is this a bard before I see me?'

To which the barman lifteth the bard from the bathwater and threw him out, damned sot!

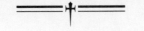

I last saw the bard later that evening at his favourite fast food outlet, Macbeths, where he ordered:

> Fillet of a fenny snake
> In the cauldron boil and bake
> Eye of newt and toe of frog
> Wool of bat and tongue of dog
> Finger of birth-strangled babe
> Ditch delivered by a drabe
> Adder's fork and blindworm's sting
> Lizard's leg and owlet's wing ...

'Would you like fries with that, sir?'

**Flacco**
**Circa 1995** AD

# WAITING FOR GODOT

## (Abridged)

*A country road. A tree. Evening.* ESTRAGON *sitting on low mound.*
*Enter* VLADIMIR.

<u>Scene 1</u>

VLADIMIR:     Hi, Estragon.

ESTRAGON:     Hi, Vladimir.

*Enter Godot.*

BOTH:   Hi, Godot.

*Curtain.*

# FOR THE TERM OF HIS UNNATURAL LIFE

*OR*

## THE TAMING OF THE SCREW

This translation was first performed on 13th July, 1608 at the Piccadilly Theatre in London. Unfortunately the theatre was not built for another 260 years with the result that this debut performance was held before an audience of two Clydesdales, a neutered kelpie and nine ferret pelts worn by Angus O'Donnel, a local merchant who abused the cast constantly and threatened physical violence if they did not exeunt his premises immediately.

## Act I

*A prison cell. Upstage right a barred window. Centre stage is dominated by a Royal Doulton vitreous china toilet bowl.*

<u>Scene 1</u>

GODOT's *head slowly emerges from within the toilet. He surveys the scene. After seventy-four minutes two guards,* ROSENCRANTZ *and* GUILDENSTERN, *enter.*

ROSENCRANTZ:      *(to Godot)* What are you doing here?

GODOT:      I'm waiting for Vladimir and Estragon.

*Pause*

GUILDENSTERN *flushes* GODOT *then exits with* ROSENCRANTZ.

*Fade.*

.........................

## Act II

*As in Act I. Night.*

*The Star Of The East hovers above the toilet. Enter* TWO WISE
MEN *and one* EXTREMELY IGNORANT MAN.

<u>Scene 1</u>

FIRST WISE MAN:  *(raising his moustache)* Who are you?

SECOND WISE MAN:  *(adjusting his lime lycra bicycle shorts)*
And where's Kevin?

*Extremely Ignorant Man blinks.*

FIRST WISE MAN:  *(looking at toilet)* OOOOOh Keith! Is that
a manger?

SECOND WISE MAN:  Well, Lordy, Lordy? Quick, Lars, have you
got the myrrh?

KEITH *and* LARS *place myrrh and frankincense into the bowl. They
turn to the* EXTREMELY IGNORANT MAN.

KEITH:                    Well, Einstein? What have you got to offer?

*The* EXTREMELY IGNORANT MAN *flushes the manger. Sounds of crying child. Enter* ROSENCRANTZ *and overzealous* GUILDENSTERN, *with batons with which they subdue the* TWO WISE MEN *and* ONE EXTREMELY IGNORANT MAN *until all three are subdued to death.*

*Slow fade.*

..........................

# Act III

Act III is interval where the audience is invited to relieve themselves on the set. ANGUS O'DONNEL hurls manure at the stagehands.

..........................

## Act IV

*As in Act III. Dusk.*

<u>Scene 1</u>

*Enter* OTHELLO *negotiating the bodies of the* TWO WISE *and* ONE EXTREMELY IGNORANT MAN.

OTHELLO:          Avaunt! Be gone! Thou hast set me on the rack. I swear 'tis better to be much abused than but to know a little ... Hark, who is't that knocks?

ANGUS O'DONNEL:    *(offstage)* Oi'l knock ye bloody blocketh off if ye daunt cease thy crappin' on!

OTHELLO:          By heaven, he echoes me, as if there were some monster in his thought, too hideous to be shown!

*Enter* ANGUS O'DONNEL, *reddened and fraught.*

ANGUS O'DONNEL:    *(gripping Othello's ruffle)* Puss off, ye lard-arsed poof!

OTHELLO:  Damn her lewd minx! O damn her!
Exchange me for a goat for 'tis of aspics'
tongues! *(embracing Angus)* All is well
now, sweeting, come away to bed.

ANGUS *headbutts* OTHELLO, *who slowly bleeds to death downstage left. Enter* ROSENCRANTZ *and* GUILDENSTERN, *who set upon* ANGUS *with sundry Tai Chi lunges which prove no match for* ANGUS's *four-by-two ironbark sleeper.* ROSENCRANTZ *and* GUILDENSTERN *die ingloriously upstage right.* ANGUS *trips on an* EXTREMELY IGNORANT MAN, *fatally connecting with the toilet seat. All cast remain motionless on stage for four days until a passing shepherd alerts police.*

*Curtain.*

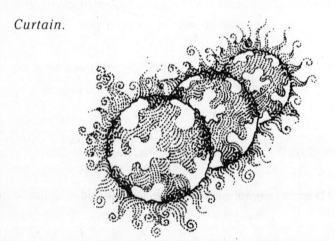